D1506565

Long Story Short

Nancy Easter Shick

Long Story Short

Nancy Easter Shick

Graphics by Frank Scott
Cover Design by Harry G Wenzel

Mayhaven Publishing
Mahomet, IL 61853
United States of America

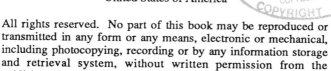

Cat Bowl Ad courtesy of Faith Mountain Catalog, Sperryville, VA
Copyright © 1990 by Nancy Easter Shick
Graphics © 1990 by Frank Scott
First Printing 1990   10 9 8 7 6 5 4 3 2 1
Printing: Phillips Brothers, Springfield, Illinois
Binding: R & R Bindery, Virden, Illinois
ISBN 1-878044-01-X
Library of Congress Catalog Card Number 90-63709

Dedication

For

Elma Cole Easter, my mother

and

Marjorie Tefft Hutton, my friend

Acknowledgements

I would like you to know that all the stories within are based on fact and any resemblance to real events and places and actual people, living or dead, is absolutely intentional and not coincidental.

I would like to express appreciation within the pages of this book to the following people:

For giving me their time and their trust and for allowing me to add to, take away, and rearrange at times, their childhood memories, I thank my father's brothers and sisters: Clara Easter Kibler, Holly 0. Easter, Ray Easter, Ralph Easter, Mary Jane Shriver, Annabelle Thompson and Bill Easter.

To the first readers of my stories for their invaluable responses, I thank my husband David; my children, April Stout and Mitchell and Lonnie Shick; my aunt, Gerine Easter; my friends, Marjorie Hutton and Sara Gray; and two of my former high school teachers, Mrs. Louise Brock-Jones and Miss Helen Harrington.

Also thanks to Sara and Joshua Easter, my niece and nephew, whose roots include Hawaii as well as Illinois. Their presence in my life this summer and their assistance with research caused the exploration and writing of the bittersweet stories of our family to seem more sweet than bitter and renewed and deepened, for each of us, our pride in being Easters.

Thanks to my son-in-law Kevin Stout for the sacrifice he made in sharing with me, his portable computer. And thanks to Rose Talbott and Sue Ellen Garner for a last minute research of dates.

For an enlightening botany lesson and a delightful stroll on Lots 114, 115, 116, 117 and 127 of the Original Town of Charleston, I thank my neighbor, Dr. Wesley Whiteside.

And finally, thanks to Doris for inviting me to the dance.

Author's Notes

For a long time, I was a listener and a reader. My writing consisted of letters, daily journals, dream diaries, recording local history and a few stories that jumped almost by themselves from mind to paper.

Many times in my listening and reading and researching, I would happen upon untold stories so emotionally powerful that I would feel a need to see them molded into some permanent form. It seemed to me that great story possibilities existed all around me.

I began to save these story possibilities. They came in many different shapes. They manifested themselves in the form of old newspaper clippings, diaries, letters, even tombstones; sometimes they were spoken words that floated around in my mind and would not go away. It was not long until I had a room full of files, notes, newspapers, tape-recordings, photographs and what seemed like hundreds of stories that needed told. I kept them carefully preserved for the day I would meet a writer who would, as I had, see the stories within.

A series of events which occurred in my life a couple of years ago, combined with an increasing number of birthdays celebrated, gave me cause to re-examine the clutter that had built up, inside and outside, during fifty years of living. It was a time for throwing away and a time for keeping. It was a time for deciding what it was I thought important enough to do for the rest of my life.

Part of my re-evaluation included opening the door to my memories and to the spare-room-turned-archives where sat the would-be stories and words I had earlier considered important enough to save. In twenty-some years of saving the material I had come across no writers, no one, who had the interest I had in seeing the stories written. I considered what should be done with all those stories that lacked only a writer.

Then the words came to me. They had been there all along but I had ignored them. "He who cares the most should be the one to do it." This has long been an unwritten law in our household. Whoever had the most fun on an evening out had to take the baby-sitter home; whoever was most bothered by pieces of lint on the floor got out the vacuum; whoever wanted a picture hung used the hammer and nails; whoever cared about keeping family and friendship ties initiated events which strengthened those ties; and so on. It is a simple rule; a good rule. It puts the responsibility on the right person and serves to remind us that we can control only the motivations and priorities of ourselves, never anyone else.

Whoever cares the most. . . !

I thought about this rule that had been a part of my life in every other area but in the area of the stories I had wanted written. It had been like knowing something without really knowing it. Now the knowledge stood in front of me and demanded that I do something about it or change my ideas about what is important.

So it was that I opened the door to my memories and to the archives room and went in. So it was that I began to do something about it.

Whoever cares the most. . . !

I care about these stories. I hope you will too.

Nancy Easter Shick
October 17, 1990
White Brick House, Charleston, Illinois

Table of Contents

Night Tidings

'I had a dream which was not all a dream.'

Byron, Darkness 1

I awaken suddenly from the dream and look slowly around the room searching for well-known shapes and familiar shadows. I wait in the darkness for confusion to exit and clarity to enter. Rectangles of light shine through the slats of the balcony's wooden shutters and illuminate the face of the travel clock. It is four in the morning and I am on the outskirts of Paris in the small city of Versailles.

I leave the unfamiliar bed and the warmth of the down comforter to sit near the light from the balcony window, second-floor, Hotel De France overlooking Louis, the Sun King's Palace of Versailles. I hear the occasional vehicle along the boulevard in front of me and I hear the scratching of the pen on paper as I write. No other sounds; it is still. The tangerine glow of lights from the parking lot create shadows like old lace through the two rows of chestnut trees that separate the hotel from the palace. A fat gray cat meanders on the cobblestone street below looking for whatever a French cat looks for at that hour.

It is a dream about my mother that has awakened me. And as always, in my dreams of her since her death two years ago, she is sitting in the kitchen of her house, the house of my childhood on north Eleventh Street. It is fitting that she is in the kitchen because it is hers in the way things become forever a part of those who love them best. Even now, though the kitchen sits abandoned with its cracked linoleum, the pattern scrubbed away by undaunted everyday battles against dirt; its walls, layered year after year with white paint now yellowed; even now, it is hers.

I am not surprised to see her in this dream and that is what makes it different from the many other dreams of my mother. I usually greet her with child-like happiness and with wonder as if it is all unexpected; as if even in the place deep within where dreams are born, I know I am not experiencing reality. While part of me, in past dreams, found joy in her presence, part of me knew it was fleeting and that only in dreams was it possible; only in dreams could the awful finality of her leaving, never to return, be changed.

But this time, I am convinced, is different. The reality of her presence is too strong, too overpowering for it to be a dream. "It is not a dream," I tell myself, from deep within the dream. "The other times were. Maybe. But this time she is here."

In the kitchen, my mother moves from the table to the stove in the northeast corner of the room. I stand across the room, my back to the dining room doorway to the west, facing my mother and the rising sun shining in the east kitchen window. I have not yet discovered why directions, north, south, east, west, are important but I note them in this dream as I have in others. The feelings I experience seem important—much more so than the details of the conversation we are having. Outwardly I am passive, but inside I am alert as if I must not miss out on anything, as if I have but a short time to watch and learn.

The dream changes abruptly in the way that dreams do, and my mother's old neighborhood friend, Della, is now standing next to her. My left

4

brain fills in what my right brain has left out—Della, slightly bent, hurrying over the path worn grassless by frequent crossings from her kitchen to ours, her quick rap on the screen door and her ritual greeting, "How do, Miz Easter." Raising her voice on the last word of "Come in?" she asks the question to which she knows, already, the answer.

They stand together now, facing me from across the room, my mother and Della, each an arm around the other, their backs to the open kitchen door. This is the first time I have witnessed an outward show of affection between them although their friendship throughout life was strong and mutually dependable. Their unity at the open door gives me a sense of protection from the world outside. There is conversation but I am more observer than participant. The words, again, seem unimportant. What is important is that the bridge of love and warmth created by the sound of their voices spans the dimensions of my mother's kitchen, and of time and connects me to them. I am safe again in a world where love does not have to be earned.

In the hop-scotch manner of dreams, though I do not see him enter, my father is now in the kitchen. He looks young and strong. His thick, coal-black hair combed high above his forehead and his straight black eyebrows make his high-boned, thin face look all angles. I do not know if I say or if I only think, "The sharpness outside defends the softness inside." It is as if my father has stepped from the old photo taken when he was in his twenties, one I have seen many times in the black-paged album my mother kept in the back bedroom. My happiness at seeing him is edged with sadness because I see now what I, after all the years of looking, failed to recognize. I see age-old pain hidden behind the young gray-green eyes. He goes to where my mother and Della stand and he joins in the conversation, sprinkling and lightening the atmosphere with banter and joking.

Others come into the kitchen, my brothers and sisters, relatives and family friends. Soon the kitchen is crowded with people and alive with sounds, as it once was. But over the heads of the others, I concentrate solely on my mother, Della, and my father, and they talk only to me. Their conversation becomes animated as they tell me of a party, a celebration they have planned for the 17th of October. I make note of the date, two weeks from today, so as not to forget. It is at this moment I awaken, confused in the transition from the familiar to the unknown. It is at this moment that I seek light to capture with words on paper this message from the night.

Already many of the details are fading but what remains strong and overwhelming is the feeling of warmth, love, and connection to my past, to my mother. And what is present that has not been there since my mother's death two years ago is the sense of peace and certainty that the connection is not broken, will never be broken; that she will be a part of me forever. It is a truth that has eluded me till now.

"What are dreams?" I ask myself, as I have so many times before. I spend one-third of my life in this sometimes less-than-tranquil land of slumber, where during the course of a year, close to 2000 of these late-night picture shows present themselves for my viewing. I cannot bear to think they are worthless, floating fragments; leftovers from the day and the past. And they have proven not to be, for me anyway, a gift of prophecy as the ancients believed. I wonder, though, about the date, so specific, so concrete, for the celebration mentioned in my dream, and I think that I must work to break the code before I can realize the significance of October 17th. While I believe it will turn out to be of importance somehow, I do not look for events of great magnitude to occur two weeks from today. I file it away in the anteroom of my mind, a puzzle for which I will later find the missing piece. October 17th. For now, it will remain a mystery.

I am a dreamer of dreams, a catcher of dreams. They seem to me, not something outside trying to get in, but rather something inside trying to get out. They bring me, often, what I need most when I most need it: insight, humility, excitement, warnings, humor—these tidings in the night.

In words from the *Talmud*, "Dreams unexplained are like unopened letters." Tonight, in a strange land, in a place far from home, I opened a letter and found a certain peace; found comfort and joy. Tonight, I went home again for awhile.

Propagation of Trumpets

"A land and the people hold memories;
they keep old things that never grow old."

Carl Sandburg

*T*his is a 'who, what, where, when and how the weather was' kind of story. If you are a reader whose mood is set on a fast-paced story that keeps you riveted to your seat with suspense, or a story that sets you down among mysterious and exotic landscapes, perhaps you should stop right here. Lay the book down.

If, however, you are in the mood to take a short and somewhat sentimental journey from past to present in the life of a small town and its people, I invite you to read on. This is a simple tale which documents the life lived on one spot of earth in that small town. It is about that most certain of all qualities of life—change. And it is about that most uncertain quality of life—endurance.

Diana's Story

I look around me and see that I, and the trumpet vine, are all that remain of my past. Far too many days of my last forty years have been spent standing over freshly-dug graves, and wearing black. I have outlived ten of my eleven children, my husband, my treasured friends and my few enemies.

But still, the sun shines on the yellow roses that grow next to the red brick outside my front door and I am able, at ninety-three, to live alone by my own hand.

I came here in the fall of 1832. The trumpet vine was planted the first spring we spent in this raw uncivilized country. Mr. Harrison Norfolk, my husband, and I had not yet moved into the two-story, hand-hewn, log house that was being built for us but he took the roots of the trumpet vine, which he had dug from the clay-colored dirt on our farm in the Wabash country, and planted those roots in the rich, black soil on the north side of our future home.

I had wanted magnolias and azaleas. "The best I can give you," said my husband, "is trumpets and roses." I was homesick for the deep south and for the ease and plenty which had been my lot the first nineteen years of my life, and I longed for anything that would give me cause to remember.

Mr. Norfolk, practical man that he was, said the trumpet vine was hardy like the Illinois prairie land which was to be our new home and would be better suited to the harsh climate of this country than would the delicate magnolia and azalea. "And roses," he said, "will grow where ever there is someone to care for them."

It was a perfect autumn afternoon when the Terre Haute to Shelbyville stage loaded with all our earthly possessions, my husband and myself the only passengers, lumbered through the mud streets of the rude settlement. The sight I saw through the open curtains of the coach window was made to look all the more ugly by the dazzling October sun. It was enough to cause me to consider insisting that Mr. Norfolk turn us around and head back south to the Wabash country. And I would have done it, too, if the circumstances we'd left behind us had not been so dreary and if the traveling to reach this place had not been so arduous. Relief that the swaying and jolting of the stage coach had lessened, seemed, at that moment, stronger than my dismay.

The words, bone-tired, took on new meaning for me. Never had I been so weary. There was no part of me that was not heavy with aches and exhaustion.

We had been riding various mail stages for five days, and for one hundred miles, from our former home on the Wabash, where I'd gone to live as a bride. The last fifty miles had taken almost twice as long as the first because of heavy October rains and the frightful condition of the roads, some of which were scarcely more than wagon tracks.

When I had almost given up hope of the journey's end, the swaying and bumping came to a halt and I pulled myself up from the thinly-padded leather seat and opened my eyes. I saw the coach had stopped in front of a raw log building that threatened to fall, and may well have, if it had not been leaning against another equally flimsy log structure. Across the street, in the middle of a square of land, men in rough garb were clearing brush and trees.

A loud blast of noise sounded out but my body and mind were too tired to react with alarm the way they had when I'd first heard the sound. We had ridden with this driver since Terre Haute and he was but repeating, with great vigor, the action he had taken at every small settlement and wayside inn which the stage had stopped the last three days.

At the blast of the stage driver's trumpet, there came running from the thickets and the handful of log buildings, men and young boys dressed in the home-grown clothing of the frontier.

They clamored around the driver, asking for news and letters from the people and places left behind.

"Mr. Moke, is this it?" asked my husband, sticking his head through the window to speak to the driver. His calm, soft voice belied shock at our surroundings. The driver did not answer until he'd climbed down from the high wooden seat and attended to the business of securing the horses, then made his way back through the mire to open the door for us. "Is this Charleston?" my husband repeated.

"Yes, sir, Mr. Norfolk. We have arrived," he answered. "Collom's tavern here's the only hotel in town. If you're lookin' for a more permanent place to stay, you might go look up Mr. Morton over at the post office. That's another block west. Be stoppin' there to throw off the mail soon as I get you unloaded. Morton has some pole cabins near by he lets free to folks settlin' here, least ways 'til they get their own built. Usually full, but it won't hurt to ask." Mr. Moke was a big man who'd spoke little, and smiled less, during the three days of our traveling with him. Now the words came from his mouth in torrents like the rain we'd encountered the last few days. "Uncle Billy Collom runs the inn here. He'll be able to tell you more what's goin' on. Better plan on spendin' the night here, I'd say." With those last words, he began lifting our trunks from the coach, and I watched as he sat them in the mud that covered the small board walk in front of a rough-lettered sign that read, "Eagle Hotel, Wm. Collom, Proprietor."

I was too tired to speak, too numb to cry. On Mr. Norfolk's arm, I made my way through the mud, with my thoughts focused only on a solid place where I could lay my head and sleep; a place that was not swaying and jolting.

14

The next morning, over breakfast of greasy eggs and fat bacon, washed down by strange-tasting tea, I spoke to my husband about my wish to find better lodging. "Mr. Norfolk," I said, when the greasy dishes, with the half-eaten food still on them, had been removed from in front of us. "For five nights we have shared sleeping quarters with strangers. I don't believe I can abide it one more night. Is it possible we'll be able to find something today, a small cabin of our own, perhaps?"

Mr. Norfolk looked at me, sympathy in his soft gray eyes, and patted my hand. "Mrs. Norfolk," he promised, "You shall have your own home before nightfall."

But Mr. Norfolk was not a magician and the best he could come up with was a mean log hut which stood northeast of the town square, then being cleared for the construction of the new courthouse. On the corner, next to the log hut that was to be our temporary home, sat a rough frame building which was used as a groggery. We moved into the hut and during our first month of living there, I looked for and found, not a rumor of culture, nor a pretension of civilization in the whole town.

In December, after we had lived in the log hut for two months, Mr. Norfolk purchased lots, from the county commissioners, on which he planned to build our future home. The wooded lots, 116, and 127, were in the second block south of the town square. Later, he would purchase adjoining lots, 114, 115 and 117. There were, at that time, 155 lots that made up the original town. In the middle of Lot 127, south of where we planned to construct our house, flowed a small stream which my husband found practical and which I found romantic, as it reminded me of my girlhood home. At this time, a log jail stood on the lots near the stream. Across the street from the jail, stood the first log courthouse but both would be moved or torn down as soon as the new courthouse construction was completed in the center of the town square.

That winter of '32 proved to be one of the worst on record in these parts and throughout those bitter-cold months, the snow and sleet and the temperatures fell, along with my hopes and my tears.

On Saturdays, the rough people would take a notion to come to town and proceed to get drunk on the grog sold in the frame building next to our log hut, then go to fighting and raising a terrible ruckus. "Such a country! Such a country as I am now in!" I would moan to myself or to anybody within earshot. Then I would run into our hut, cover my ears, and cry over the change from the life I had known in Natchez to the awful ways of this Illinois country.

"Mr. Norfolk, are you sorry that you have married me?" I would ask, when he came home tired to find his dinner either half-cooked, or raw, and me in tears. Feeling sorry for myself consumed much of my time in those early days and many times my husband would walk in the door, tired and hungry, to find no meal ready. And sometimes no meal at all might have been better than the food I set before him.

Mr. Norfolk had opened a store; the first real store in the village, and he was working hard to make it a success. He was the kind of man who felt it necessary to do his social and civic duty and he had much to keep him occupied. There was plenty that needed doing in those days to aid in the growth of the young town.

He never grew angry at my self-pity and my ineptness at cooking and cleaning. Before I had married, my life had been feather-bed soft. My two half-sisters and I, in our family home in Natchez, were taught absolutely nothing about the labors involved in home-making. I knew neither how to cook nor how to do laundry. I had not needed to know because in Natchez, we had depended on slaves for everything.

"What you need is a tutor," said my husband, and he went out of the house in search of one, with the determination and self-confidence that had caused me to, eight years earlier, take notice of him.

Eight years earlier, in 1824, I was in my 19th year and living in Natchez, Mississippi, far from Troy, on the Hudson, where I was born. My folks left New York when I was but an infant and joined with thousands of others who were looking to better themselves. We became part of what is now known as the great westward migration.

A lot of changes occurred in my life in a short time. We moved first to Ohio. Another move took us further west and south to Natchez, where most of my childhood was spent. My father died, and my mother soon after remarried. During the next few years, I acquired a half-brother and two half-sisters. You would have thought I'd have learned early that change was a rule of life rather than an exception. But it was an easy life, full of laughter and idle pursuits, and I thought that it would always be so.

In that year, 1824, my sisters and I were invited to the annual cotillion held at a plantation near the river. I was reluctant to go because I had been to those affairs enough to know that women outnumbered the men by a large margin, and competition to fill a dance card was fierce. Like every properly brought-up southern girl, I knew how to cast down my eyes, and flirt behind my fan, but I suppose I had too much Yankee in me to play the simpering southern belle. It went against my grain to trade pluck for guile and a full dance card.

But my youngest sister wanted badly to attend the cotillion, as it would be her first, and Mamma would not allow her to go unless I went. As it turned out, if I had not gone, I would never have met Mr. Norfolk.

I saw him across the large parlor-turned-ballroom and I smiled because his appearance was so out of place among those elegant cut-away frock coats with tails that reached to the back of the striped-trousered knees—the required dress for southern gentlemen on such occasions. The slightly-built man whose eyes met mine from across the room wore a bob-tailed coat which at one glance told that he was no dandy. Such garments were usually worn by the less sophisticated: young boys, clerks and preachers, or the like.

The minute his eye caught mine, he made his way with dignity and directness across the room to where I was standing. I forgot about the sleeves of his frock coat, which in spite of his slight stature, stopped a little short of his wrists. I, instead, took note of the ease and authority with which he moved across that crowded dance floor. His manner caused people to move back automatically to give him room. "I would feel safe," I thought, "following that man anywhere." Our eyes still holding, I touched my young sister's arm and whispered, "I have found the man I will marry."

He stood before me, slightly shorter than I, and I said not a word but held out my dance card. When he handed it back, the name "Harrison R. Norfolk" was written on every line.

Before I went home that night, Mr. Norfolk had asked permission to call. I had found out that he was a traveling man, three months younger than I, who, though born in Maryland, had grown up with relatives in Cincinnati. With Mamma's permission, he began to call at our house. A short time later, he asked me to leave my life of ease, and go with him to search out the land of milk and honey. The merchandising firm he worked for in Cincinnati convinced him the place to search was in the Wabash country of Illinois.

What we found, when we arrived in the Wabash country, twelve days after our wedding, was a poor log hut and meals of corn pone and fat bacon. And ridicule at our city ways!

"What's that girl got on her head? Is it a steam-boat or what"? mock-whispered the girl in the home-dyed, linsey-wooley dress. The other girls broke out in a fit of giggles as Mr. Norfolk and I walked down the rough planks that served as the aisle of the Newlight church. It was our first attendance at 'meeting' in the Wabash country, and as a bride, I was fixed up pretty well. I had on a fine new leghorn bonnet of delicately-plaited straw that had cost $15. We girls down south did know how to put on some style, and I was proud of my hat and my new green muslin gown with the leg o' mutton sleeves.

My face turned red at the impudence of that girl's remark and I fumed during the entire service because when the people weren't shouting and praying, they were turning in their seats to stare at us. When we returned home, my anger turned cold and the first tears I had shed, since I was a child, came. " Mr. Norfolk," I declared through my tears. "I will never, ever go to church again in this dreadful country." He said not a word, just held me close, comforting me until my tears and my anger, abated. I kept my word. I never returned to the Newlight church.

We lived on a small farm on the Wabash and my husband continued in merchandising and though he was successful in all his ventures, we were not happy with the lawlessness of the place. Then an event occurred that shortened our stay in that country. Mr. Norfolk was asked to be a candidate for sheriff, and to both our great sorrow, he was elected. "What if you have to hang someone?" I asked. He shook his head, as if bewildered by the predicament he was in. It was the first time I had seen indecision in him. "You weren't even able to kill that chicken last Sunday for dinner."

"I have some friends up near the Grand Prairie, in the new county of Coles," said Mr. Norfolk. "Got a letter from them last week telling me of great possibilities which abound there." So he resigned his office of sheriff, and that is how we came to Charleston.

When I first heard the name of the village that would be our new home, I had visions of brick houses, beautiful gardens and a genteel people, the name having such an established southern sound. It was not until much later that I found out the town was not named for its southern sister but for one of the men, Charles Morton, who had given the land upon which the town was laid out.

Mr. Norfolk was true to his word that he would find me a tutor. The day after I had filled the hut with tears over the fighting and drinking created by the groggery and over my inability to be of much use in this country, my husband reminded me that we would not live in the log hut forever. And he brought home the farmer's wife who was to become my tutor. It was she who taught me to wash and cook.

The first thing the farmer's wife did was show me how to make soap. "Save your ashes and your grease," she said, "and make your soap in wintertime." I was a good student. It was a lesson I would repeat religiously for sixty-five years—until this past year in fact. Last winter, in my 92nd year, before I could get out the grease and get on with the job of making my usual fine kettle of soap, I became afflicted with the grip, and had to buy store-bought soap for the first time. Doesn't do the job my home-made soap does, but I can get used to it if I must. I've encountered plenty of changes over the years, and most of them have taken a sight more getting used to than changing to store-bought soap.

By the summer of 1834 when we moved into our new log house—the finest residence in town so the local newspaper said—the trumpet vine, along with a black locust and an American beech, seedlings my husband had brought with us from the southern part of Illinois, had been planted and were growing with promise. I felt more hopeful than at any time since leaving Mississippi as a bride. The old log jail still sat between our new house and the town branch, as we had come to call the stream. But Mr. Norfolk reassured me the new courthouse in the middle of the square was almost completed and when it was, the jail would be located there. Then the whole block would be ours.

I was learning, from the farmer's wife, to become more useful. I could now make soap and do laundry as well as any other wife on the Illinois frontier. And I had learned to cook; could make decent corn cakes, though I was convinced I would starve to death before I learned to like them.

It was a good time in our lives. The first of our eleven children had begun making their appearance, so I had plenty to keep me busy. And I was well-satisfied with our log home which was the envy of all who saw it.

Most helpful of all, in making this wilderness truly the land of milk and honey for me, was two women I came to know that grew to be my dearest friends. Through them, I found that culture and civilization did, indeed, exist in this place, and long before the day I arrived.

Mrs. Margaret Monroe was the wife of Byrd Monroe, and they moved here from Kentucky a few years before we came. Mr. Byrd Monroe had been trained as a doctor but pursued a life in business after he moved here. He was an enterprising man; did a little bit of everything from being in state and local government to operating mills and successful merchandising establishments. There seemed to be nothing beyond his capabilities, and Margaret was just as talented. Oh, I admired her so! She could do anything she turned her hand to, weave, spin, crochet, cook; even helped Mr. Monroe teach their children Latin and the classics. Many is the time she, in her generous and lovable way, helped care for the sick or gave to those in need. No woman in this town ever fulfilled their mission in life better than she.

To have been blessed with one true friend is as much as a person could hope for in a lifetime. But I was fortunate in having two. The second was Mrs. Dr. Ferguson—Susan. She was a daughter of Charles Morton and had come to this place before the county was formed. In fact her marriage to Dr. Ferguson was the first one on the record books in the new county. In the long hours of my grief when death began making too many unannounced visits to our household, Susan was at my side. Long after others admonished me to get on with life, she sat beside me, sharing and understanding my sorrow.

No strawberry friends, who show up only when the fruit is ripe for harvest, these ladies! I have found it to be a most precious thing; friends who will share the joys, as well as the sorrows handed to us all by life. For me, their friendship made the prairie winds blow a little softer; the trumpet blossoms smell a little sweeter.

We spent several years in our pioneer log house and during this time, Mr. Norfolk's fair dealings, and mind for business brought us prosperity. One day a team of oxen and a flat-bed wagon pulled up in the street in front of our home, loaded down with a contraption the likes of which I had never before seen. Mr. Norfolk and the driver lifted the black metal box with legs, from the wagon, and carried it into our house. "Mrs. Norfolk, you will be the first woman in town to make corn pone on a cook stove." said my husband. He had traded the bacon and produce, which he and the driver had hauled overland to Chicago, in return for the stove. "But wait," he said. "I have something even better for you." And he went back out to the wagon. When he returned, he had in one hand, a deed for the two-story brick house that stood two doors north, in the next block. In the other hand he had a yellow rose bush, its roots protected by a bright-patterned gingham cloth.

It wasn't long until we moved into the two-story brick house which had been built, shortly after the brick courthouse had, by Mr. James Alexander.

It had been the first brick residence in town. The trumpet vine, which I had come to cherish every bit as much as I had the magnolia and the azalea of my youth, now covered much of the north side of the sun-bleached log house. It had become, as had my friends, a symbol of hope and comfort in a harsh land. I could see it from the front door of my new home. Its presence there seemed to make my connection to the log house stronger and I felt no need to transplant the roots to our new house. Instead, I planted the yellow rose bush outside my front door and today it yet lives, spreading alongside the red brick. A peppery aroma and a splash of yellow greet me during the months of May and June, when I walk out the door.

Lately, I find myself looking toward the south often; toward the mass of flowers and foliage that cling to the side of the log house, our first real home here in Charleston. The deep green leaves and the soft orange of the trumpet blossoms never fail to connect me to a past that I was, often, too busy to appreciate. What I would give to have back some of those hours! No, I never tire of the sight of the trumpet vine.

Through the years, I watched as the log house became home to others. Watched as the house was enlarged and a porch added. Watched as the trumpet vine grew fuller.

Captain John Eastin and his family called the log house, home, after we moved out. Captain Eastin and his bride Jennie, came to this place before we did, when it was yet a settlement. The Eastins told us about an experience they had the first Sunday after their arrival here. They went to church all rigged out in their wedding finery and their new store-bought clothing created a sensation. They weren't laughed at the way Mr. Norfolk and I had been down on the Wabash but the next morning before breakfast, six men came to Captain Eastin to borrow money for purposes of buying land. The men concluded the Eastins must be wealthy from the extravagance of their dress. Truth was, they had but $6 to their name. Captain Eastin reached prosperity quickly though, after coming here, as he was a brilliant and hard-working man. But he had an eye for horse flesh and a weakness for gambling on it, so it was said, and was known to have won and lost several fortunes in his lifetime. I have heard rumors that he became the owner of the Lots and the log house when a horse and a rider he imported from Kentucky won a close race over in the Ellington pasture. They were good neighbors, the Eastins, and took good care of the house and the trumpet vine.

Several families moved in and out of the house after the Eastins lived there, and over the years, the Lots were split up and sold to various people.

It was the Gramesly family who lived in the log house during its final years. And it was young Marie Gramesly who loved the house and the trumpet vine as I had.

By 1877, the trumpet vine covered the whole north side of the log house. That was the year it became home to Charles Gramesly and his bride, Keturah. I watched as they moved their new wedding furniture into the old log structure. And I watched, three times, as Doc Patton rushed past carrying his black satchel, to help bring into the world the three Gramesly daughters. Marie, the third daughter born, made her appearance in the house in 1887.

I watched as Marie grew from a babe to a child. I watched as she played in the shadows cast by the trumpet vine on the old house. The root sprouts of the vine had by this time curled around the northeast corner, framing the window of the bedroom where Marie slept. I could imagine the sweet smell of the trumpet and the sound of the wind through the leaves, whispering to her as she slept there, in much the same way it had whispered to me. It is through her, the legacy of the trumpet vine lives on.

I am now in my ninety-third year and the weight of the years, and the past, lie heavy on me. Everyday, I see pieces of my past disappear, like amber beads on an old necklace, which age has worn thin the string. I watch as the string breaks, and one by one, the beads fly off, and are lost. There are very few beads left now.

I could not watch, at first, when they began to tear down the old log house last summer. Ten-year-old Marie stayed with me that day. She could not watch either, though she was excited about the new house that would replace it. "Just think," she told me. "Ten large rooms, and hot and cold running water!" And like her, I marveled at the thought.

I was determined not to cry too long over this latest loss. It has been a hard lesson for me, over the years, to refrain from clinging too hard to the past. One consolation for me, and for Marie; the trumpet vine will be saved. By and by, it will bounce back from the shock of upheaval and workmen's boots and will grow strong again to cover the north side of the Gramesly's modern, brown-shingled, Queen Anne house.

Having young Marie around has kept me from growing old too soon. She keeps me informed on what great things are happening in this world today and I am her connection to yesterday. "Marie," I told her when she brought over her school studies on the presidents. "Do you realize that Abraham Lincoln passed this way many times in the '40s and '50s? Why, Uncle Billy Rigby's blacksmith shop was just over a block and Mr. Lincoln was often there, renting a horse, to ride out to Goose Nest Prairie to see Aunt Sally. She raised him, you know, after his mother died. Wasn't always fond of Mr. Lincoln's politics but I did admire the way he treated his step-mother!"

"Pappa tells the story of how he sat on the fence at the fairgrounds and listened to Mr. Lincoln debate Mr. Douglas." said Marie. "Pappa had moved here only the year before. Was fifteen at the time! I know all about Mr. Lincoln before he became president. I should! " she added. "I've had to listen often enough to Pappa's stories."

The noise the men were making in tearing down the log house came through the open parlor window. It seemed to be taking such a long time. Suddenly it seemed worse not to be there when the end came for the old house. I looked over at Marie and saw that she was listening to the noise also. "Perhaps we should check. . . " I said. She nodded her head in agreement and old though I am, she reached the door only slightly before I did. We reached the corner just as the last of the hand-hewn, log boards fell to the ground. We watched as the two old brick fireplaces with their tall chimneys—all that remained standing—became rubble.

Marie's Story

"What I remember best," said the small, gray-haired lady in the wheelchair, "about my childhood, is the trumpet vine which grew up the side of the old log house I was born in." Her hands clutched her father's diary and the stack of photographs which lay in her lap.

The volunteer historian, who was gathering information for the county history book compiled to celebrate America's bicentennial, sat in a chair beside her, listening to the soft voice recite precisely the stories of early Charleston. Seeing the past through Marie Gramesly Reasor's sharp eyes and strong sense of proper, made it come alive for the historian; gave the historian a sense of being there alongside the young girl, Marie.

"When I was about sixteen, Pappa sold land south of the town branch and an opera house was built there." There was a glimmer of pride in Marie's voice. "It was exciting to see all the vaudeville troupes come to town and perform there.

The year before, Mr. Woodson, who then owned the lots north of our house, sold them to the city for a public library and a park. My oldest sister, Margaret, was one of the early librarians there. I liked having the opera house on one side of us and a houseful of books on the other."

A sadness crept into Marie's voice as she went on to tell of the old log house being torn down and of the Queen Anne house being built in its place. And then of the Queen Anne house, so modern in 1897, being torn down too, and replaced by the building which would house the Elks lodge.

"It's difficult to drive by and see the trumpet vine no longer there," she said. "As if it never existed." As she talked, the historian had the feeling that the trumpet vine had imprinted itself on her childhood no less than the photographs taken by her father, which showed a young Marie with thick braids and a sprinkling of freckles across her nose; Marie in a white pinafore sitting with her friends on the fence in front of the old house; Marie playing in the yard near the trumpet vine.

"Many times after I left home in 1909, and was married, I would go past that house and be comforted to see the trumpet growing there as it had when I was a child." Marie smiled at the memory. The smile left her face, as she went on, "I thought I could not bear it when the house and the vine were torn down. It's been over twenty years since it happened, and it's still a shock for me to be driven down Seventh street and find nothing from my childhood left." Marie closed her eyes and her next words created a vision the historian would not soon forget. "When I close my eyes, I am there, a child again, standing in the shadow of the old log house and the trumpet vine. I can yet smell the fragrance of those trumpet blossoms."

The volunteer historian used the information passed on to her by Marie about the young village of Charleston in the bicentennial history book of the county. And she never forgot the story of the trumpet vine. Later, when she thought of the story and the effect it had had on her, she put the words on paper and she told the story and showed the photographs of Marie and the trumpet vine to her grandchildren. She could not let the story be lost. She took them to the place where the old house and the trumpet vine once stood, where the library and the Elks building now stand. And the library, and the spot where Diana and Marie had lived much of their lives became a part of the lives, and the memories, of her grandchildrens' childhood.

Brittany Anne's Story

The small girl, blond pony tails bouncing, held her mother's hand as she walked alongside her up the steps that led to the library. "This is where Grandma takes us," she announced. "I think Abraham Lincoln drank water from that water fountain there. And over there," she said, pointing to the south of the library, "was a log house. Grandma told us all about a woman named Diana who lived there." There was excitement and pride in the small girl's voice at being the knowing one. "And she showed us pictures of a little girl named Marie. Marie lived in the log house, too, once upon a time. Wasn't any cars in those days. Just horses!"

The small girl stopped and turned around. She paused as her eyes searched the silver maple tree which stood at the edge of the grass, growing almost onto the sidewalk in front of the library. When she found what she was looking for, she smiled, knowing that she had saved the best for last. "Mommy, do you see the vine growing up the tree there, the one with the pretty orange blossoms. That's Diana and Marie's trumpet vine!"

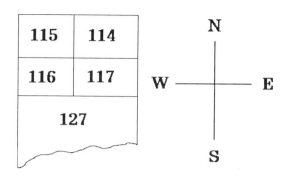

Where

1690—Part of the French Claimed Territory/Louisiana
1750—New France
1774—Annexed to the Province of Quebec
1783—Claimed by Virginia
1784—Northwest Territory
1790—Knox County of the Northwest Territory
1801—St Clair County of the Northwest Territory
1809—St Clair County of the Illinois Territory
1812—Madison County of the Illinois Territory
1814—Edwards County of the Illinois Territory
1816—Crawford County of the Illinois Territory
August 26, 1818—Illinois becomes a state
1819—Clark County of the new state of Illinois
1823—Lots 114, 115, 116, 117 and 127 becomes part of
       Edgar County
December 25, 1830—Coles County
September, 1832—Resurvey of the town: Lots 114, 115,
       116, 117 and 127 becomes part of the Original
       Town of Charleston, Illinois, County of Coles

31

Longitude   *11 West*

Latitude   *40 North*

Above Sea Level *669.208 feet, according to the bench mark put there by the Department of Commerce, U.S. Coast and Geodetic Survey in 1935.*

North Of *a murky little stream flowing west through the town, known by all who have lived here, as the town branch. The town branch which has its headwaters—if a gushing word might be used to describe a trickle of water—in the northeastern section of the township of Charleston. It trickles south, turns and meanders west and gathering strength from its journey through the town, heads off—slightly more energized now—to converge with Cossell and Riley Creeks. Cossell Creek is probably better known in the area of its confluence with the town branch as Dunn's Creek, though the name exists in the memories of the ageless boys who fished and played here and will not be found on any map. Both Cossell and Dunn were early land owners at some point near the creeks, hence the names.*

There are two answers, in case you ask the question, as to how Riley Creek got its name. More interesting, but less likely, is the answer given by country lawyer, A.C. Anderson who wrote his reminiscences in 1939. He says it was named for James Whitcomb Riley, neighboring Indiana poet, who was a frequent visitor to Charleston. Probably closer to correct, is the explanation by the writer/compiler of the 1906 Coles County history, C.E.

Wilson. He gives the honor to an early settler named James Riley who was here and gone long before the poet Riley came to visit.

The area where the story takes place is also a couple blocks north of Southern Street, which is now known as Harrison, and north, ten minutes by foot—if you walk at a brisk clip—of Old Main, built in 1896 as the first and foremost structure for the new Normal school, now Eastern Illinois University.

South Of Chicago, Champaign, Camargo and the Coles County courthouse square. Directly south of South Street, now known as Van Buren.

West Of Indianapolis, the Wabash River, the former site of Uncle Billy Rigby's blacksmith shop and the Coles County jail, on which spot once sat the house and law library of Alexander P. Dunbar, the town's first lawyer and desk-mate of Abraham Lincoln in the 1844-45 Illinois state legislature.

East Of St. Louis and the Mississippi River. Also east of West Street, now Fifth Street, which runs alongside the west edge of Lots 114, 115, 116, 117, and 127. Fifth Street once bridged the town branch and went south to meet Southern (Harrison) Street but now dead-ends before it reaches the waters of the town branch. Also east, nine or so miles, of the city of Mattoon, Illinois.

Down beneath the Kentucky blue grass, crab grass and dandelions that today cover the soil on the Lots, is 50 to

200 feet of layered glacial material brought down from Canada during the ice ages. Beneath the glacial debris is sedimentary rock formed when an ocean covered this spot. And even further below the earth's mantle and outer and inner core is Tatsaitan, Mongolia, if one has the patience, desire and where- with-all to dig.

Up from roots that have found a home in the black soil; growing upward through the unseen gases of nitrogen, oxygen and argon and through the invisible but some-times-felt particles of water vapor, dust and pollen that make up our atmosphere, are resources of nature which reflect the past and the present.

What

Natural Resources Six black locust trees, non-native to this area, grow here. The black locust has a tendency to send out roots close to the surface of the ground as far as forty or fifty feet from the tree, producing new trees. These six are, most likely, children of those original trees whose seedlings arrived in this place by design, hand-carried and planted 158 years ago by early settlers. The bark on the old trees is dark, deeply ridged and cross-hatched, the wood strong, hard, and durable. In late spring, fragrant white flowers grow in clusters on the trees. Of the six black locusts on the lots now, two stand on Lot 115 behind the library. Two stand down near the town branch close to the sidewalk. Two stand in a bramble patch of trees, plants and weeds near the town branch in back of the doctor's office on Lot 127.

Growing within this same bramble patch are several trees of heaven. These natives of China were brought to the United States by way of Europe shortly after the Revolutionary War. They did not catch on in popularity in central Illinois or in Charleston until the late 1800s. Fast growing, these trees of heaven, their seed wings fly through the air and easily sprout new trees in new places.

Also in the bramble patch, with the black locust and the trees of heaven, are mulberry, hackberry, box elder, Siberian (Chinese) and American elm. Immigrant trees from Eastern Asia, Europe and neighboring Southern States grow alongside the natives in this place. Together they stand, largely unnoticed, around the gravel parking lot like mourners gathered around a gravesite; survivors huddled close for comfort.

Boston ivy climbs up the ridged bark of the black locust that stands near the back north side of the library. And in the bedding plants on the southwest side of the building, a black locust sprout, escaped from its parent tree, pushes its way up through the earth affirming the black locusts ability to multiply and survive.

Two silver maples, natives to the area, grow near the library; one on the east next to the sidewalk was probably planted at the time the building was completed in 1904. The other on the northeast edge of the building looks to have been planted later, perhaps around 1918.

Clinging to the silver maple planted next to the sidewalk is the thick, gnarled vine of the Campsis Radicans—the trumpet flower—an escapee from the original trumpet vine planted by the Norfolks in the 1830s.

Older plantings around the library include a horse chestnut tree, a hackberry, an American elm and three sugar maples. A hemlock, probably planted after World War II when it became popular to plant shrubbery around houses, grows in front of the white bungalow style house on Lot 127. South of that, in front of the 1950s style white, moderne building which was converted to a doctor's office in the 1960s, stands a middle-aged, fast-growing sycamore.

Newly planted near the stone water fountain which sits, shaped like a tree trunk, in front of the library, is a thornless honey locust. A white, ornamental Chion-anthus Virginicus, or fringe tree, grows near the honey locust. Thomas Jefferson, said to be fond of the fringe tree, planted the small trees at Monticello, There are also two Bradford pear trees. Originating in China, these trees have only lately come into fashion and are grown for ornamentation, not fruit. At the front south corner of the library is a red leaf form of sand cherry, More a shrub than a tree, the sand cherry comes from the great plains.

Once, not so many years ago, a large one-hundred year old plus American beech stood in front of where the Elks building now stands. The American beech does not normally grow west of the beech border which extends across central Illinois near the Paris-Grandview region. This particular beech first stood in front of the Norfolk log house, digging its roots deep into the earth about the time of the Civil War.

Man-Made Resources

Norfolk log house—1834 · 1897

Gramesly Queen Anne house — 1897 · 1954

Carnegie Public Library building —1904 · present

Peterson Park brick and concrete arch —stood on the northeast corner of the Lots. Torn down, ca. 1960.

Tree-shaped water fountain —similar in shape and style to gravestones produced by Alexander Briggs who had a monument shop in the next block north. Date of construction unknown.

White Bungalow — 720 Sixth. Built, ca. 1926

White Art Moderne house —730 Sixth. Built, ca. 1949; by Jay Montgomery. Remodeled for use as Doctor L. E. Adkins' office, ca. 1960.

Elks building/Senior Center — The Elks lodge and bowling alley was built in 1954 on the site of the old log Norfolk house, later the site of the 1897 Gramesly Queen Anne house.

Charleston area senior citizens began sharing the building with the Elks in 1978.

City of Charleston Water Tower — Built in 1952 by the Chicago Bridge & Iron Co.

Who

Early Inhabitants *No names of the Indians who once dwelt in this area have been left for us to roll around on our tongues except that of a chief named Ka-Ne-Kuk, who was described as a 'fine looking specimen of the noble red man. . .' Ka-Ne-Kuk went into trances whereupon visions appeared to him; visions which he would share with his people during what the settlers referred to as preachings. A member of his tribe, Black Beaver, is also known to us by name. He is said to have killed a warrior whose name is not recorded. Black Beaver lies buried in J.W. Brown's pasture in Ashmore Township, a few miles east of Charleston. We do not know if Chief Ka-Ne-Kuk or Black Beaver ever put bare or moccasined foot on the Lots by the town branch in the Original Town of Charleston. But with the coming and going of the Kickapoos, Pottawatomies and Kaskaskias through the area, and with the Indian encampments which existed when the settlers first came here in the 1820s, it is probable that at least one of the early inhabitants walked near the town branch and stepped foot on the Lots.*

Benjamin Parker *(1788-1836) was the first person to own the land on which Lots 114,115, 116, 117, and 127 are located. He is given credit for building the first cabin and planting the first orchard in the town. To recite the Parker history is to tell a long story so perhaps all* that needs to be told on these pages about Parker is that he was a member of the 'Preaching Parker' clan, recognized as the first permanent settlers in Coles County. How permanent they were is up for debate as many of them headed southwest toward the territories of Texas early in the town's history. Some of the Parkers, possibly to their everlasting regret, made it to Texas, but that, again, is another story. There is conflict in written records as to whether Benjamin was one of those who reached Texas or, as one source states, made it only as far as Missouri. Most likely Benjamin never lived on the Coles county land which includes the Lots that he purchased from the government for $1.25 per acre in 1829, and of which twenty acres he gave for the new county of Coles. Another early settler, **Charles Smith Morton** (1786-1848) also gave twenty acres and together, the forty acres were used to locate the county seat which began the Original Town of Charleston. It is known that Benjamin Parker left and Charles Morton stayed, and that may be why the town is called Charleston and not Benjaminton.

Thomas Sconce was the surveyor for the Original Town of Charleston, which included 99 Lots in the first survey of April, 1831. In the resurvey ordered in September, 1832, the town was enlarged to 155 Lots.

Isaac Lewis built the first log jail which sat on Lot 127 from 1832 until 1835 when it was moved inside the new courthouse on the town square.

Harrison Richard Norfolk *(1805-1866) purchased Lots 114, 116, and 127 in 1832, on which he built a two story hand-hewn log house. He and his wife,* **Diana Miller Norfolk** *(1805-1898) lived in the house several years. Their children:*

Richard Norfolk
Charlotte Norfolk Parcels
Edwin S. Norfolk
Ellen Norfolk Wallace
Ezra Norfolk
Harrison Norfolk
Elizabeth Norfolk
Henry Norfolk
Josephus Norfolk
Inos Norfolk
Louise Norfolk Wingate

Captain John Michael Eastin *(1808-1892) lived with his family in the Norfolk log house in the 1860s. He was the son of Major Charles Eastin, who was the first white male child born in Kentucky. Capt. J. M. Eastin came to Coles county about 1830 with his bride,* **Jennie K. Reed Eastin** *(1809-1890). Charles S. Morton was his second cousin and the Eastins lived for awhile with the Mortons upon their arrival here.*

Dr. Jewell Davis *(1811-1884) had his home and office on Lot 114. Born in Ohio, he was, at times, a farmer, cooper and carriage maker before an illness in his family propelled him into the study of medicine. He came to Charleston in 1854 and practiced medicine here, and though having studied various systems previously, he* confined himself to no particular method. Dr. Davis had an interest in bee culture and kept about a hundred colonies. He invented the queen nursery for propagation of queen bees.

E. E. Buck Merchant and former editor of the Charleston Courier, he sold the Norfolk log house to Charles Gramesly in1877.

Charles Gramesly (1842-1925) and wife **Ketura Hildreth Gramesly** (1856-1949) and their daughters were the last family to occupy the Norfolk log house. Charles was a man of many vocations and advocations, among them businessman, farmer and amateur photographer. Their children were:

Margaret Amidon Gramesly
Phebe Hildreth Gramesly Marvel
Marie Sayre Gramesly Reasor

Captain Abner M. Peterson (1825-1890) The park on Lots 114, and 115 was named Peterson Park for this man who was a physician and later an attorney. Born in Pennsylvania, he came to Illinois in 1849, and to Charleston in 1863. He was a Captain in the Union Army under then Colonel Ulysses S. Grant. Peterson was also mayor of Charleston and a county judge. He donated money to the city of Charleston for a public park. Several surrounding towns also have parks named for Peterson as they too received park fund money or land from him.

Henry M. Hackett *He and his sister Eva Soper lived in the white bungalow at 720 Sixth Street during the 1930s, 40s and 50s.*

Marshall F. Newman *lived in the Queen Anne Gramesly house until he sold it to the Elk's Lodge in 1952.*

James Woodson *was the proprietor of the City Mills in the 1890s. He and his wife, **Margaret Hall Woodson**, lived in a house that sat in the northeast corner of the Lots. They sold, in December, 1901, one-half of Lot 114 and all of Lot 115 to the city of Charleston for $4,000 for park and library purposes. The city purchased the other Lots later.*

C. E. Wiley *(1862-1912) son of **Eli** and **Martha Wittemore Wiley**. He was born in Charleston, graduated from Yale, was an early president of the library board and helped secure money from Carnegie for the library building. Upon his resignation and departure from Charleston in 1902, it was noted that "The [library] building will stand as a monument of his interest in his native city."*

Andrew Carnegie *donated $12,000 to the city of Charleston for the building of the library. A city ordinance changing the name from Charleston Public Library to Carnegie Public Library was adopted January 2, 1902. Construction on the building began in 1902 and the library was opened to the public January 15, 1904.*

Lizzie Purtill *first librarian in the Carnegie building which opened in 1904 with 2844 books.*

Sheryl Snyder *Library Director at Carnegie Public Library since 1976. Sheryl is the overseer of 49 thousand items available to the people of Charleston and is, along with Katie, Kirstin, and Alexandra Stout and Brittany, Ryan, Andrew and Daniel Shick, current keeper of the legend of the trumpet vine.*

Litany of
Childhood Days

"*M*innie Minoso is my father, he is, he is, my uncle is," (whatever that meant), boasted a kid named Blue from Chicago. He had come to spend his summers in the countryside with an aunt who lived next to the cornfield a block from our house. Upon seeing our baseball card collection, (my brother Dan's and mine) he tried to impress us with his superior knowledge about baseball, gained first-hand, from living in a two-big-league-baseball-team-town. We weren't easily impressed. We thought him strange. What did he know? He was, after all, a White Sox fan.

It was summertime in the 1950s and summer was baseball, even to two kids in a small midwestern Illinois town with the closest big league baseball park 130 miles away. We told ourselves, not without pride, my brother and I, that we were the only Yankee fans in our town, maybe the whole county, perhaps even the whole state. It would have not been so unusual if it were true. New York was 900 crow-flying miles away and in those pre-tele-vision (at least in our neighborhood) days, seemed a thousand light-years from the flat prairies of central Illinois.

But my brother and I were readers, and into our young hands had come the stories of the New York Highlanders-turned-Yankees, of Babe Ruth, and of Lou Gehrig. And with those tales, into our hearts to stay forever, had come the love for anything connected with blue pinstripes. It hadn't hurt that during those formative years, an old legend named Joe, who roamed center field in the white gingerbread-trimmed arena called Yankee Stadium, was getting ready to move over to leave space for the creation of a new legend from Commerce, Oklahoma named Mickey.

My brother and I lived and died with the Yankees; loved every player who put on a Yankee uniform; studied the team photos and memorized the players' names and faces, even the bat boys, (Eddie Carr and William Loperfido in 1956), mourned when a player was traded; disdained the constant meddlings of the front office. And we did what every non-playing, baseball-loving kid did in those years. We collected baseball cards. With the daily shuffling and rearranging and trading of those cardboard rectangles, the names and the faces of the men on them etched themselves deep into our souls.

Almost forty years it's been, and still the heroes of yesterday march cadence through my mind. The months between the last game of the World Series and the first game of spring training can seem like forever to a baseball fan, and that old proverb about absence making the heart grow fonder rings true, instilling longings and casting reflections within. So it happened that one winter's day, the rhythm of those familiar names from an earlier era danced over and over in my head, then jumped from my head to my pen to a piece of paper. I gave the words, a gift of love and remembrance, to my brother Dan who shared my childhood, and my baseball cards. And together, we give them to all who knew baseball in the fifties.

Magic days they were. Warm, summer days that forever haunt our memories. Phil Cavaretta, Cavaretta, Cavaretta. The name rolled so smoothly on our tongues. His playing statistics might have been mediocre but his name was big-league all the way. Harry Chiti, Chiti, Chiti. As close as we could get to a forbidden cuss-word in the presence of our mother.

Nellie Fox, forever with a wad of tobacco in his jaw. Joe Ginsberg (Danny, Danny Joe Ginsberg) forever ugly. Baseball in the 1950s, forever ours.

Litany of Childhood Days
[Or When baseball cards were six for a nickel]

In my mind will always be
their names just like a litany.
From hazy, lazy, childhood days
when baseball cards were all the craze.

I close my eyes and there are traces,
suspended in time, cardboard faces.
Marching before me, now they come,
our heroes mixed with bubblegum.

Dom, Dom, DiMaggio. He's not as good as his brother Joe.
And Whitey Ford can beat Preacher Roe.
Luke Easter's our relative, did you know?
There was Spahn and Sain, then pray for rain.
Piersall, Kluszewski and Ferris Fain.
Sal the Barber, quiet Hank Sauer,
Say-Hey Willie, stone-faced Hank Bauer.
Stan the Man and Elroy Face,
Mickey Mantle next to ole' Case.
Enos Slaughter, Johnny Kucks, Allie Reynolds,
Virgil Trucks,
Teddy Williams, Roy Campanella, Phil Rizzuto,
Bobby Feller,
Harvey Kuenn & Al Kaline, Rocky Bridges, Ronnie Kline,
Bobby Shantz, Tommy Byrne, Early Wynn, Jim Hearn.
Dusty Rhodes, we can't forget. Hoyt Wilhelm
and Lew Burdett
Yogi Berra, Stan Hack, Suitcase Simpson, old Joe Black.

I must confess, I must reveal,
I dream of baseball when the grass was real.
If I could re-live, I'd choose no other
than those days shared with Dan, my brother.

Born in the Sign of the Foot

*E*mma Knock was born when the sign was in the foot. At least that's what her Rardin, Illinois neighbors laughingly said about her. Because everywhere she went, she walked. The truth is, Emma was born when the sign was in the head—in the sign of the Ram, Aries—if you go by the Farmer's Almanac. The date was April 14, 1878. The place was a two-story frame saltbox house built by her father, a few miles south and east of what would later become the village of Rardin.

She grew up on the land—part prairie and part timbered hills—bordering the Embarras River. The land had been first claimed by Emma's Golladay ancestors in 1832, when they migrated from Virginia to Illinois seeking the land of milk and honey. It was on this land in a log cabin, the forerunner to the frame saltbox of Emma's birth, that Emma's mother, Mary Golladay was born.

Emma's father John Knock, German-born, had come to Illinois with his family when just a child. Soon after their arrival in America in 1843, the Knock family made their way westward settling in Charleston, the county seat of Coles County, which lay thirteen miles south of the Golladay settlement.

The Knock men were skilled craftsmen; some were gun-smiths and some were carpenters. All were workers of wood. All of them, regardless of their vocation, were at one with the land and with nature, and everything around them blossomed and grew. When John Knock married Mary Golladay and moved to the Golladay homestead, the land—part prairie and part timbered hills—flourished under John's skillful and devoted care.

Emma, the sixth and youngest child born to John and Mary Knock, grew up in the years before the turn of the century on that land of milk and honey her ancestors had settled, and on which her father labored and prospered. Emma's mother died when Emma was four. From that time on, her father became the most important person in her life. It was from this simple, hard-working man of nature that she learned to work hard, speak the truth and revere the land, especially to revere the land. Emma learned early in life to care for the land and for the creatures on the farm. She learned to cook for the hired men who came to help plant and to help harvest the abundant crops that grew in the fertile prairie soil. She learned to plant a garden, to reap and store the bounty. She gathered the fruit from the orchard and the berries and nuts from bushes and trees, and made ready for winter and for the time when food might not be so plentiful. She used the ways handed down to her by her father and his father before him, those who had come from Germany. And she used the ways from the Golladay side of her family, some of whom, legend has it, had been waiting on shore to greet those first pilgrims seeking a better life. She learned which mushrooms were safe to eat in the springtime and how to, in late winter or early spring, catch the sap running from the sugar maple trees in Knock's Holler. She learned to waste nothing, to be self-reliant, to live from the land.

Seasons came and went and chores varied with the changing seasons. There was a rhythm to life and a satisfaction in keeping pace with that rhythm.

In 1881, when Emma was three, men of vision, knowing the Clover Leaf Railroad would be built nearby, created the village of Rardin. It was their dream that their town would become a great city. And Rardin did thrive, for awhile. The village reached its peak in the early 1900s, then slowly turned into an always Sunday kind of town—another small village whose promise was never kept.

In her early years, Emma and her family could get almost anything they needed in Rardin. When the town's growth dwindled, the Knock family turned more often to Charleston, the county seat and trading center.

Emma's world was not large; she never traveled far. One of the great events of her life, one that she would tell people about in her later years, was the time she turned sixteen and left Knock's Holler with her father for a trip to the big city, to Springfield, Illinois. While there, she had the portrait made which later hung above the fireplace in the parlor. From an oak frame, a young Emma, raven black hair and high cheekbones, gazed with piercing blue eyes, upon all who entered the Knock home. She was a pretty one, that youngest child of old John Knock.

Yet, Emma never married. She'd come close once. She'd promised to wait for him when he went off to fight in the Spanish-American War. He never returned. As the years went by, she never much dwelled on his death except to say once in a great while, "I promised him I'd wait. I'm still waiting."

Perhaps the greatest tragedy of her life occurred when her father died. From that time on, she had to love the land enough for both of them.

She became the care-taker of that land—part prairie and part timbered hills—bordering the Embarras. At first in grief, later in pleasure, she walked alone the path she and her father had walked together. She stopped to rest where they had stopped to rest, roamed the woods in Knock's Holler, over-saw the boundaries of the land to see that nothing was amiss. She explored the remains of the old sugar camp, paused along the banks of the river where in former times, travelers had forded the Embarras or patronized her Grandfather Golladay's saw mill. And the rhythm of her life went on.

She continued to care for the land and for the creatures who inhabited it. She would allow no harm to come to either. She continued to plant and harvest and repair and make ready for winter. Never one to sit idle, when the weather kept her inside, she would sit by the fire on the couch she called old hillside, sorting through hickory nuts or walnuts gathered and cracked earlier, packing the nutmeats into jars. She even popped corn, storing it in sealed jars, ready for eating on nights when the cold winter wind kept her inside. She believed in being prepared; she could survive off the land. Her father had taught her well.

Across the road from the Knock house, almost hidden by the surrounding grove of timber, was the cemetery that had been deeded to Morgan Township by Emma's Golladay ancestors. What had begun as a small family burial spot had become the final resting place for many of her neighbors and friends. To the south and the east of the cemetery, the land dropped sharply, forming the ravines, and beginning the hills and hollers that rolled on to the river. Tall cedars, pointing heavenward, had been planted among the tombstones by her ancestors.

The cemetery fell under Emma's steward-ship also. She felt an obligation to be there for every burial. She would stand near the entrance, holding a bouquet of wild flowers or blossoms from her garden, and greet those coming in the gate with a "Hi ya!" Her greeting was always the same. If snow and ice covered the ground, she broke off twigs or small tree limbs for people to stand on, keeping their feet from contact with the cold ground. Practical Emma!

Although Emma lived a somewhat solitary life, she had a warm nature and thrived on contact with those she cared about. When loneliness got the best of her, she would walk into Rardin or the thir-teen miles into Charleston. Her "Hi ya!" was a welcome sound to her many friends and relatives.

Life was not all work and no play for Emma. Music was her great joy. And she was surprisingly musical for someone who had no formal training. When her chores were done for the day, she would play the piano or her harmonica, or both at the same time, the harmonica held by a strap around her head. On days when the sign was in the foot or otherwise, Emma could be seen, harmonica in hand, traveling the dusty dirt roads into Rardin or Charleston, or somewhere in between. While wait-ing in stores or at the courthouse or at friends' or relatives' homes, she would entertain herself and others with her music. Once it happened that her harmonica developed a flaw.   One of the notes ceased making music. She was able to afford a new harmonica but making do was part of her nature. When playing a song that called for that particular note, she simply improvised with her voice, never missing a beat.

It was well known that Emma was a little different from her sisters and brothers. Most people thought it was a good difference. One day, she motored into Charleston with one of her sisters, who not being born when the sign was in the foot, got around mainly by automobile. While at the bank, Emma waited in the lobby for her sister to complete her business with the bank's president. Never one to just sit, and thinking to entertain herself while waiting, Emma got out her harmonica and began to play a spirited tune. The sister, hearing her from the inner office, blushed and began to apologize. "Oh, that Emma!" she began, shaking her head.

The bank president smiled, "Ah, everyone knows Emma. Don't worry about it. Besides, I like it."

Emma was Emma. One of a kind.

I can't remember a time when I wasn't familiar with the name 'Emma Knock'. She was my father's first cousin, once removed, on his mother's side—the Golladay side. In his growing-up years, my father and his family had lived nearby on one of the Knock's tenant farms. Later, as a young man, he had worked for Emma on her homestead. My mother knew and loved Emma too. Her childhood had been spent in the Rardin area and Emma was a special friend of the family. There was no lack of 'Emma' stories around our household. I was seven years old when I first met the legend behind the stories.

She whirled into our house one day and immediately created a flurry of excitement. She brought with her a charge of energy that lasted long after she had gone. To my child's eyes, she looked like an Indian, tall and lean, her skin weathered brown from days in the sun. She was in her sixties then, but still she could kick her heels higher than her head. She did just that, on this day, simply to prove she could.

Age had not yet faded the piercing blue eyes. Quickly she focused those eyes and that energy on me, determined that I should learn to play our old beat-up and out-of-tune piano. Her energy was boundless but her patience was not. So I, not completely without guile, diverted Emma's attention to one of my mother's other children, one more musically inclined than I.

I never did learn to play the piano, though Emma could not be held responsible. That day, she entertained us with music from her harmonica and from the piano and with her conversation. But the thing that stood out most in my mind was the intensity of her presence. She was as alien to me as if she had come from another world. She was like no one I had seen before, no one I have seen since. Even now, many years later, I have only to think about that day to realize again that sense of energy she created.

After that first memorable visit, Emma's trips to Charleston appeared to become more frequent. I loved those times, and better yet, I loved our visits to Knock's Holler. Life went someplace when Emma was around. She shared with us the knowledge of her years. She shared with us the joy of her living. What was her secret, this magic lady? I didn't think about it much then. I just accepted it and took delight in it. I think about it a lot today. I had never met anyone before and I've never met anyone since who generated in me the type of feelings that Emma did. She embraced the past while living completely in the present. No one could get as much pleasure out of a moment as could Emma. She knew who she was and she accepted what life handed her unless she thought she could improve it. Then she tackled what needed to be changed with unlimited determination. She was a curious mixture of challenge and contentment. In the eyes of the world, her life would probably not be judged a success. But then, as now, my eyes beheld a successful woman.

In the early 1950s, Emma, though ill herself, walked to Charleston for the funeral of my grandmother. It was to be her last trip to town. She knew her own death was close at hand. Her wish was to be buried on the land of her birth—part prairie and part timbered hills—bordering the Embarras River. Her wish was to be buried just inside the gate of the Golladay-Knock Cemetery. She wanted to be there to greet the people as they came in.

She told all she came in contact with of this wish. But still she worried that her instructions might not be followed, at least exactly as she wanted. So one night, barely able to get up from her bed, she left the two-story frame saltbox house built by her father, and she crossed the country road to the cemetery with the tall cedars pointing heavenward. In her arms, she carried an empty milk can and a shovel. Sitting on the upturned milk can, this woman who had lived her days at one with the earth, turned the soil—dug her grave one shovel deep—to mark the spot. She wanted to make sure there would be no mistake, to satisfy herself that she would always be there to greet those who came; to be there to say, "Hi ya!" to all who walked through the gate.

Sometimes when life's cares seem too much; sometimes when my spirit is in need of being lifted—I get in the car and follow a country road north to where the land is part prairie and part timbered hills. I drive the road that winds back and forth along the Embarras River until I come to the top of a high hill, then turn east and stop at the

small tree-surrounded cemetery. I pause just inside
the old iron gate and say, "Hi ya!" to Emma.

By The Bird's Song

'Hark, by the bird's song, ye may learn the nest. '

Tennyson,
Marriage of Geraint

*T*rouble seemed to stalk Clara Mae like a lean, hungry cat stalks a baby bird. It seemed she was forever in the wrong place at the right time. By the spring of 1924, when I was fourteen and Clara was ten—the first spring after Mom had gone—Clara and adversity had developed more than a passing acquaintance.

We lived in the little brown house of Matty Shafer's on Walnut Street that spring, just a few blocks over from the Vine Street house—the only house we'd ever owned—or almost owned. The Vine Street house was where we were living when Dad and Mom...when Mom left. Guess Dad's heart just wasn't in stayin' there after that and it wasn't long before we'd moved to Walnut Street.

But that's another story. One I haven't figured out yet. Sometimes, don't think I ever will. The only way I have of makin' sense of things is to take them out of my head where they whirl around day after day, and put them down on paper. Someday I'll write about the night Mom left. But not now. Not yet! This is mostly Clara's story, I guess. Though, all us kids have a share in it, and it's hard sometimes to separate one person's story from another's.

I had my hands in the chipped blue bowl, mixing the biscuit dough the way mom had taught me. Good thing she had, as it turned out. Mom and Dad both insisted that we all learn how to do things around the house. "Out in the yard, or out on a job,"

Dad would tell us boys, "that's not all there is to takin' care of a home." Dad had been a bachelor a long time before he married Mom and I always figured that's why he felt so strong about us learning how to cook and clean.

"Hands were made before spoons, Earl," Mom would say when I would shy away from getting the wet floury, biscuit dough mess all over my fingers. "And don't overwork it after you get the shortening mixed in," she would remind me.

My hands were deep in the lard and flour mixture when I heard a noise from the bedroom which I knew was the baby. "Annabelle's awake," I thought, "but she must be all right. At least she's not crying." I had changed her diaper before I put her down for a nap in the afternoon. "Now, Annabelle, if you'll just wait till I get these biscuits made. . ."

The kitchen door slammed and I looked up to see eight-year old Ralph standin' there. "Ralph, pump some water in the washpan and fill the tub out back. Looks like you've been over at the tile factory pond again. Holly with you?" I looked up from the bowl and toward the door for a sign of five-year old Holly. "Need to get that clay washed off your feet. Dad'll be here shortly and he'll be tired and hungry." Ralph didn't say anything. Just got out the washpan and began pumping water into it.

I went on. I knew I had a tendency to over-talk, to over-explain but knowin' is one thing; not doin' is another.

"Dad didn't get much sleep today. No sooner got home from the gas plant when Mr. Alexander called. Seems his new filly is havin' leg problems. You know how he thinks Dad is the only one who can. . .Holly, look at you!" He had finally come in the kitchen door. Like most kids that age, he thought he was big enough to do whatever the older boys did. It looked like he had. Was he ever a mess! "You've got that old clay all over you, head to toe. Haven't missed a spot."

The only part of Holly that was free of the reddish-brown clay from Record's tile and brick factory pond was his clear blue eyes rimmed with white and a few wisps of his curly blond hair. "You look more like Hershel Calloway than Holly Orville E. Ripley Jackson Clark Easter," I said shaking my head. We all smiled at the ridiculous name. The family joke about how Holly had come close to being weighed down with that name came from happier days and was always retold when things got too serious, or I got too gruff, or we just wanted to remind ourselves that once we had been a whole family.

I turned back to mixing my biscuits. It crossed my mind for the thousandth time, how Mom had made it look so easy, the work of keeping house and tending to everything. And here, I couldn't even get biscuits made for supper. I didn't feel good about bossing the kids around so much either but someone had to do it now that Mom was gone. It looked like now—as it had from the beginning—that the someone was gonna be me. Not that I minded. I did feel bad about missing so much school. I loved school and that other world I had come to know through books. Right now, though, it didn't seem important. Miss Endsley, the principal over at Lincoln where we were goin', was real understandin'. Said maybe things would work out and I could go on to seventh grade in the fall. There are a lot of good people in the world, I had found out. And some not so good. Those not so good do-gooders are the ones we could live without. 'Goo-dooders' Clara Mae liked to call them—sometimes to their faces too. Imagine! Wantin' us to give up the three little ones. Dad wouldn't hear of it. We're still a family. Always will be!

I turned my attention to Holly again. "You're goin' to need more than the washtub." I said. "Help him Ralph. See if you can find some of that soap Granny Golladay sent over. Where's the girls?" Now that I thought about it, I hadn't seen Virginia, Clara or Mary Jane for over an hour.

"Where's Mary Jane?" I asked Ralph. "Who's watching her?" Baby Annabelle's noises from the bedroom were threatenin' to turn into cries. I started cuttin' out biscuits, somethin' I wasn't very good at, and Ralph and Holly went back outside to wash up. Where were those girls when I needed them! Wasn't like Virginia to be gone.

"Virginia," I yelled. Where had she gotten off to. Now, Clara, that little skunk, she was always slippin' off gettin' into trouble. She'd been something of a Momma's girl and she'd been real restless since Mom left. But she was awfully good about looking after the little ones. She was always huggin' and kissin' them and given 'em lots of attention, things kids that age need. If she wasn't in a mood to tease 'em!

The front screen door slammed, and Clara, black hair flyin', came swirling in quickly through the front room and into the kitchen. Reminded me of the dust devils I had seen in old man Monroney's cornfields late last summer. We were living in the Twelfth Street house then, near the northeast edge of town. The place where all the trouble started. "Clara, get. . ." I began, but she was already at the old wood cabinet, moving the handle of the pump rapidly up and down causing the water to come gushing out, missing the washpan that sat there, and splashing all over the floor. She made a pass at washing her hands in the splashing water; made another pass at drying them off on her skirt.

Ralph came through the back door, clean now, and he stood and watched her. "Good thing Dad isn't here to see that," he said grinning. Clara made a face at him as she flipped, in his direction, what water remained on her hands. She opened the metal cabinet to get the dishes out and began setting the supper table.

"Well, I guess there is such a thing as miracles." I said with mock surprise. Clara shot me a quick look and a smile that made crinkles at the corners of her gray-green eyes, and lit up her small face. Before she could give me a smart answer, we heard Dad's whistlin'. We three stopped and listened, waitin' for the sound of his footsteps. We could always tell when Dad was near. He didn't whistle the same tune every time but we all knew his sound. Same thing with his footsteps. They had a lightness and a rhythm to 'em that nobody else's could duplicate. Something about his stride and the way his shoes hit the sidewalk, I guess. Clara and Bill claimed to be able to know Dad was coming from two blocks away but I don't know. . . they have a tendency to exaggerate now and again, though both have had reason to be on the alert for his sound often enough.

The tune Dad was whistlin' this evening was familiar but the way he was whistlin' it was not. In fact we'd all heard Dad sing and whistle *My Gal, She's a High Born Lady* a hundred times or more but this evening it sounded more like a funeral dirge than the Irish jig he usually turned it into.

Bill came in the kitchen at that moment. He was eleven and usually took advantage of the free-dom that came with being a little older and largely unsupervised, except by me. He stood still, listenin' to Dad's whistle, then shot me a look which told me he agreed with my silent assessment of the nature of Dad's tune. "Someone's on the southpaw side of Dad tonight, sounds like," he said. "Glad it's not me."

We both took a look at Clara's face. She would not return either of our glances, and I knew, most likely, we would not have to look further for the source of Dad's wrath. "O.K., Clara Mae, what did you do?" I asked.

"I. . . " she started to say something and then froze at the sight of Virginia coming through the kitchen door, her head down and her cheeks wet with tears. Bill and I looked at each other again, both of us with surprised expressions on our faces. Neither of us could believe that Virginia was cause for the funeral dirge sound.

Dad, carrying one of his keen switches and a frown, walked into the kitchen right behind Virginia. Mary Jane, a scared look on her face, toddled in after him. Dad's step was light but his shoulders, under his still crisp-looking white shirt and red suspenders, slumped with weariness. It couldn't be easy, I thought, to come home tired and have to take care of the needs of nine kids, one of those a babe in diapers plus all the household chores. Of course I was there to help and Ray, the oldest at fifteen, had helped some when he wasn't working at the shoe factory.

A few months ago, though, Ray had talked Dad into signing the papers for him to join the army. "Unheard of!" Dad had said, "Not even sixteen yet! Always knew you were the one with wanderlust, Ray, but you don't know what you're gettin' yourself into. You're too young to remember the war. All those young men goin' away hometown heroes and comin' back bums! No jobs, no way to live."

We knew he was remembering the broken young men he had brought home with him, the ones who came through riding the freights. He came in contact with a lot of 'em, what with the gas plant bein' near the crossing of the Clover Leaf and the Big Four railroads. When we lived in that house across from the gas plant, he would show up with hungry men several times a week until Mom put a stop to it. "George," she'd say, "We don't have enough for us and the kids. We can't feed everybody that's hungry." She felt sorry for them too, she told Dad, but us kids came first.

Once in a while, the only thing those had-been soldier boys needed was a warm place til the next train came through or their spirits lifted with whiskey or song. Dad would supply one or all three, gladly.

Dad was well-known for his way with animals, his knack of doctorin' and healin' horses. Always wondered if his healin' touch had worked on that one soldier he brought home with the feet that were all crippled and swollen. Mom had cried at the sight of them. We didn't have anything in the house to put on them so Dad ran up to that drugstore on the square and bought gauze and ointment. Never saw such gentleness as when he cleaned and medicated and wrapped that man's feet. The war had been over several years, but Dad hadn't gotten over his anger at the way those young men were ignored by their country. Better not ever bring it up with Dad if you don't want an argument.

Anyway, Ray persisted in his quest to be a soldier. More than anything, I think, he wanted any life that could be lived somewhere else for awhile. I couldn't blame him. Dad signed the papers. So now

Ray was somewhere in the Pacific, on a ship making its way to Hawaii. Clara missed him a lot. Would lay in the grass outside on that little hill behind the house, wishing on the first star that Ray would come flying in on one of those aeroplanes we'd been readin' about in the headlines of the newspaper lately.

Dad hung his tweed cap on the nail beside the sink, and Virginia, still without looking at any of us, went towards the back door where Ralph were standing. Holly had come in and was standing next to Ralph, dripping water all over the floor. Virginia fluffed Holly's wet curls and gave Ralph a smile and a hug.

Mary Jane was sticking close to Dad, clutching tightly to his trousers, her thumb in her mouth, and the scared look still in her eyes. Dad pried her small hands loose and picked her up, holding her high enough to touch the low ceiling. Mary Jane giggled as Dad began to sing-song the nursery rhyme about some Duke of York who marched his men up the hill and down again.

Clara kept her eyes on Virginia, who was now pumping water into the washpan. Virginia kept her back to Clara and began to wash up. When Clara could not catch her eye, she turned away and quickly finished setting the table. I noticed, at Virginia's place, Clara put the only plate we owned which was not chipped and the only remaining fork and knife that still matched each other; the ones that usually found their way to Clara's place at the table.

After Dad put Mary Jane down, he took charge of things and it felt like a ton of coal had been lifted from my shoulders. He began giving orders, " Holly, your feet aren't clean yet. Sis," he said, nodding towards Clara, "Hold the kerosene lamp for him while he goes back outside. Gettin' dark out there. Bill, Ralph you help me get supper finished up and on the table." Tired as he must have been, his movements in the kitchen were quick and cheerful, and brightened the early evening hours for all of us; all except maybe Clara. She was still being most un-Clara-like, trying to keep from drawing attention to herself. She wasn't pulling the lantern back behind the enclosed porch wall the way she usually did when it was pitch-dark outside and Holly was out in the yard at the washtub. On a normal evening, Dad would have yelled at least twice by now for her to quit scarin' Holly.

Dad began singing, *Buffalo gals, won't you come out tonight,* as he got out the iron skillet to fry the jowl bacon. Soon we were all workin' and singin', and movin' around that little kitchen like worker bees 'round a honey-comb.

I was in the middle of stirrin' the gravy when I heard Annabelle let out a loud cry. Poor baby. I had forgotten all about her and I guess she was lettin' me know she was tired of waitin' for someone to come take care of her. I gave the spoon to Virginia to finish the gravy and went to change and feed Annabelle.

Times like these, with all of us at home and workin' together, it was almost as if things were back to normal; as if Mom might come walkin' in from the next room. I had a feeling of what I guess might be called happiness. The sadness was right on it's heels though. I could feel it hangin' around. Because the problem was, times like these didn't seem to happen too often lately. When Dad was home things ran pretty smooth but too many times Dad rushed through supper so he could spend some time on Monroe Street with his friends before going in to work. Or didn't come home for supper at all. I pushed those thoughts away. He was here now. That's what was important. Why borrow trouble when it looked you in the eye often enough, as Ray would say.

Annabelle had been changed and fed. I had not dropped her this time like I did that scary day last fall not long after Mom had left. I had tried to warm her cold, wet bottom during a diaper changin' and had held her over the cook stove where, wigglin' and squirmin', she slipped from my clumsy and inexperienced hands. All I knew to do was put lard on her bottom to try to soothe her pain and keep the skin from blisterin'. It had healed and I had gotten better at takin' care of her since.

We sat down to eat our supper of bacon, gravy, biscuits, and a vinegar pie that Dad had whipped up in the time it had taken me to take care of Annabelle. I knew the biscuits and gravy weren't up to what Mom or Dad made. But the smells were mouth-waterin' and we were all hungry. The food would disappear fast enough, no matter who cooked it.

"Now, I want to tell all of you kids," Dad said in his I-mean-business voice. "I've told you before, but some of you," he looked at Virginia, ". . . seem to forget pretty fast." All signs of easy humor and song had disappeared and in their place was a stern, laying down of the law look that we didn't even dream of questioning, at least to his face. "I don't want you hanging around down at Miss Eveline's place." He continued. "Don't want you samplin' any of that dandelion wine or any other concoction she cooks up. I'm not sayin' she's not a good woman but that's no place for kids."

I noticed, at Dad's words, Clara drew in her breath and under lowered eyelids, looked toward

Virginia. Virginia kept her eyes down as if inspecting the faded pink rose pattern on her plate.

Nobody spoke for a moment. Then Dad started eating. The rest of the kids took their cue from him and the clatter of metal against china began. I continued to watch Clara. Her shoulders relaxed and she exhaled softly. Relief, I could tell. Virginia had not told on her.

I knew who had been responsible for Virginia being at Miss Eveline's to sample the new batch of dandelion wine. Dad, had he not been so tired, would have known too; would have realized that Virginia would never have gone to Miss Eveline's on her own. Dad had warned us all many times to stay away from there. It was clear to me that the one person in our family who thought "don't" spelled "do" was behind the whole escapade. I wondered if it was also Clara's idea to take Mary Jane, rather than leave her unwatched. It was my guess that when they all heard Dad's whistle, Clara had lit out for home. Of course, Virginia wouldn't have run, and wouldn't have left Mary Jane behind. Clara's eye caught mine and she smiled, at first sheepishly, then defiantly. She knew I had figured it out. She also knew I wouldn't tell.

Dad rose from the table and began clearing the plates. Some of us had not finished but when Dad was through eatin' he never paid any attention to whether the rest of us happened to be in the middle of a bite, or had food left on our plate. It was automatic with him. The meal was over. It was time to start cleaning up. And dishes never sat in our sink! Sometimes I wondered if he was as tired of sayin' as we were of hearin', "Dishes aren't done til they're put away." Those of us who still had food on our plates which was most of us, stuffed what we could in our mouths, furtively keeping an eye out for

Dad's left hand which would southpaw you in a minute for using, what he considered, bad manners at the table.

We boys followed Dad out to sit on the front porch for a few minutes before he lay down to catch a couple hours sleep. He had to leave for his ten-hour night shift job at the gas plant at 11:00. It was Bill, and Ralph's, and my turn to finish cleanin' up in the kitchen but Clara had insisted she and Virginia would do it tonight. We could hear the clanging kitchen sounds that meant supper dishes were being washed.

Through the open window, the two older girls' voices singing *Go Tell Aunt Rhody* lifted out into the warm night air in a clear, sweet harmony that is possible only between sisters or other close kin. I knew Clara was, in her own way, trying to make it up to Virginia for the switchin' Virginia had taken earlier; the one that had rightfully belonged to Clara. As for Virginia not tellin' on Clara, holdin' together against the rest of the world was an unwritten law none of us would break. Not then, not ever.

It was quiet here on the porch, only the crickets chirping in the grass and the sounds made by the girls in the kitchen. Dad sat in the dusky shadows cast by the soft arc light from the street corner. His head leaned back against the old brown wood of the house, and his eyes were closed but I could tell he was awake by the slow rhythm his fingers tapped out against his knee. Holly sat, his head against Ralph's shoulder, almost asleep. Bill stood against the porch post, staring out into the night. The muffled sounds coming from inside meant the girls were finishing up. Their song continued, and the third verse of *Go Tell Aunt Rhody* floated gently through the still, night air. I

joined in, singing softly, "The goslings are crying,
The goslings are crying. . . "

An Apple For Clara

*M*iss Antha Euphemia Endsley, tall frame erect, auburn hair pulled back in a neat bun, walked down the hall at Lincoln Grade School, the square heels of her practical shoes tapping a precise rhythm on the marble. The bodice of her dress was bloused loosely around her waistline in the post-war fashion but the hem of the skirt measured closer to her ankle than her knee in a statement befitting her profession rather than the style of the day. She stopped at the door of the fourth grade room, and the teacher at her desk, seeing the principal, closed her book and came to the door to greet her.

When Clara, who sat in a front row desk near the window, shifted her gaze from the cloudless blue sky, her mind from her daydream of sitting on Granny Golladay's front porch, and looked toward the two young women huddled in the doorway, she knew why the principal was talking to the teacher and who it was they were talking about. Flight was her first thought. She quickly sized up the situation. The fourth grade classroom was on the second-story of the brick school building. "Windows are too small to get through," decided Clara, though if anyone could get out through them, she, with her scrawny frame, could. What with Miss Endsley and her teacher blocking the only other exit, she rose from her desk and went toward the two women before the teacher had a chance to call her name. "No way out of this one," she conceded to herself.

Miss Endsley, her ever-present smile present, looked down at the small, black-haired girl, and without a word being spoken, they went out together through the door and down the hall. "Always got that smile on her face," thought Clara. "Bet she'd be smilin' if the school was burnin' down."

The janitor looked up from his mop at the sound of the two unmatched pair of footsteps in the hall. The sight of their shapes, teacher and child, one so tall, one so small, outlined in the bright light coming from the window at the end of the building, brought a smile to his face.

When Clara and Miss Endsley reached the music room, they turned in. Clara could see that Blanche and Pearl were already there, sitting on the piano bench. Clara stopped long enough for Miss Endsley to walk in first, then she followed, staying close to the figure of the principal. The sixth-grade teacher, Mrs. Rosebraugh, who was in the room searching among the song books, found what she was looking for and smiled absently as she walked past them toward the door. Miss Endsley's words stopped her. "Mrs. Rosebraugh, do you know we've got ourselves a prizefighter here at Lincoln school?"

Mrs. Rosebraugh stopped and looked back. "Why, no. No, I didn't." she said, " Who is he?"

"Oh, it's not a he; it's a she," Miss Endsley answered, nodding in the direction of the small girl still standing slightly behind her. "It's Clara, that's who!"

Mrs. Rosebrough's eyes squinted behind the gold metal frames of her glasses, as she peered into Miss Endsley's face to catch the meaning behind the principal's pronouncement. Assessing the situation, Mrs. Rosebraugh decided Miss Endsley was trying either to shame the small girl or put her at ease. Deciding it must be the latter, she looked at Clara and smiled, and spoke cautiously, "That's nice to know." At a loss to know what else was expected of her, she turned and walked out the door.

From the looks on the faces of the three young girls, it was the two sitting huddled together on the piano bench who needed to be set at ease. You could see the fright in the eyes of the younger sister, Blanche. The older girl, Pearl, was squirming on the bench and looking out the window. The face of Clara, who had moved from the side of Miss Endsley to sit in a chair near the wall, was stoic, unreadable.

"All right, girls," Miss Endsley began, as she produced a piece of paper from the pocket of her skirt. "I want to hear the story behind this note Blanche and Pearl's mother sent back at noon."

Nobody said anything.

"Blanche, suppose you start." she said to the younger of the two sisters. Blanche avoided Miss Endsley's eyes, instead glared at Clara as she spoke, "Clara just started beatin' up on me when we were walking home for lunch. And I didn't do anything to her!" The last few words quivered as they came out, and her eyes filled with self-righteous tears.

"I'll do it again, too," said Clara with menace, "if I ever catch you being mean to my sister, Virginia." Her fists clenched and her small body half rose from the chair.

Miss Endsley took charge, ignoring Clara's threat. "What do you mean by Blanche being mean to your sister? What did she do to Virginia?" asked Miss Endsley, looking at Clara.

Clara shot a fierce look toward Blanche who sat looking down trying to figure out, as if by braille, the lines which formed the plaid of her brown cotton dress. She would not meet Clara's eyes. Indignant, Clara said, "Made fun of my sister's dress! Said it looked like it was from welfare.[1] Then slapped her hard in the face just cause Virginia told her it looked good as hers. Nobody's gonna do that to my my sister cause she never fights. Wouldn't hurt nobody, ever! She. . . " Clara said, jumping up from the chair again and shaking her finger at Blanche, "didn't have no right to slap Virginia. And Virginia's dress is ever bit as good as hers. Wasn't welfare."

Clara's voice softened on the last words and she slumped back in the chair. Her eyes wondered around the music room and found, hanging on the wall, a new picture next to the old ones of Lincoln and Washington. She stared at the shy, unsmiling eyes of the new President, Calvin Coolidge, and as his eyes stared silently back, she added in a low husky voice, "Not that one anyway. It's one Mom made."

Miss Endsley's mouth tightened, and she clasped her hands behind her back to keep from reaching out to touch Clara. She composed herself and went on. "Pearl, how did you get involved?" she asked.

"I come along behind them, and saw Clara on top of Blanche," answered Pearl. "I wasn't gonna let anybody beat up on my sister," she added, with the pious look of a holy avenger.

"Did you stop to think about how small Clara is and how much bigger you are, Pearl?" Miss Endsley asked gently.

---

[1]   The word 'welfare' is used in this, as well as the following story, because it may be better understood by contemporary readers. The term 'relief' was the word more often used during this period. Aid to the needy was usually provided by township and local charitable groups before the federal and state welfare programs of the 1930s went into effect.

"No, ma'am," said Pearl, looking down towards the floor. The smugness had gone out of her at the principal's words.

"Well, all three of you girls know the rules. There is to be no fighting to or from school. And all three of you broke that rule." said Miss Endsley. "Now all three of you will have to suffer the consequences."

She sighed and turned her back, got the large paddle down from the wall. "Blanche, you will be paddled first for starting the fight," she said. "And," she added sternly, "you must remember, we do not make fun of people who may be less fortunate than ourselves. I don't want to hear of you doing it again!" She turned to Pearl, "Pearl, you will go next because you had no business fighting Clara even if she was on top of your sister. Clara is smaller than your sister, and much smaller than you. And you, Clara, you know the rules. There is to be no fighting to or from school. When you break the rules, you must be punished. You know that!"

As far as Clara could see, the smile had not left Miss Endsley's face; had been there since she appeared at the door of the fourth grade classroom. Casual observers, people who looked only on the surface and never beneath, might have agreed. But those who looked closely at the gentile, raw-boned farmer's daughter, might see that her smile, or what passed for a smile, was actually a tightening of her mouth, a gritting of her teeth, and a bracing of herself for the frequent encounter of unpleasant tasks which came her way by virtue of her job as mediator and overseer of so many human beings. She was accustomed to paddling children. It was a task she did well. It was not a task she liked.

She placed Blanche over the piano bench, dress raised so as not to wrinkle it and so as not to add any cushion to the blows. She was known to wield a hard paddle. The paddle had not come down the first time before Blanche let out a scream that would curdle the milk in Mr. Dunn's dairy cattle that grazed two blocks west of the school near the fairgrounds. Miss Endsley did not soften her blows; she gave Blanche her paddling in full measure, amid the ruckus the young girl was raising.

"Acts like she's bein' murdered," thought Clara, folding her arms and turning her head in disgust.

Pearl had started crying at the sight of her sister being paddled and at the thought of being next. When Miss Endsley was through with Blanche, Pearl who was sobbing a little louder now, took her place on the bench. Miss Endsley raised Pearl's dress as she had Blanche's and lifted the paddle in the air. She hesitated a moment, the paddle suspended, at the sight of skin showing through a small round hole in Pearl's snow-white bloomers. Clara, still sitting in the chair, looked over at the suspended paddle, then down to the spot where Miss Endsley's eyes were fixed. A smile started inside Clara. Blanche, sniffing and crying, saw what the other two were looking at and quickly turned her head. The sight of her sister being paddled was humiliating enough; the sight of the hole was too much to be borne. So she chose to ignore it, and attending to her own misery, began sobbing loudly again.

Miss Endsley went on with her task, bringing the paddle down hard as she had with Blanche. The skin that showed through the little round hole began getting pink, then turned bright red as the paddling continued. Clara across the room, fascinated by the sight of the hole, kept her eyes on the skin showing through, white as the bloomers at first, then a light shade of pink, finally red like the apple she had seen on Miss Endsley's desk as they had walked past her office on their way to the music room. As she watched as the skin turned bright red, Clara thought, "Boy, Miss Endsley spanks hard." Then she grinned to herself, "Bet prissy ole Pearl will wish SHE'D been wearing a pair of new welfare underwear when Blanche tells her about that hole. Least mine don't have holes in them." The thought widened her grin, and the grin grew until it turned into a snicker. She put her hands over her mouth to hold back the snicker but the snicker erupted into a laugh. She tried to stop the laugh when Miss Endsley heard her and turned to her, saying, "Well, Clara, if you think this is so funny, just remember. You're next."

Just when Pearl thought the whipping would never end, Miss Endsley laid the paddle down, and turned to Clara. "Come here Clara. It's your turn."

Clara went to the piano bench, all laughter gone from her face. In its place was a tight 'determined-not-to-cry-and-make-a-fool-of-herself-like-Pearl-and-Blanche' look. Miss Endsley did not lose the smile from her face nor did she spare the paddle, bringing it down on Clara's bottom ever bit as hard as she had on the other two girls. When the principal had finished, Clara knew she had been paddled, but within a few minutes and without much difficulty she succeeded in convincing herself that Miss Endsley's whippin' was nothin' more than a fly swat compared to her Dad's.

Miss Endsley went to Blanche and Pearl who, in the aftermath of their trauma, still sniffling and wiping the tears from their eyes now stood near the door, eager to be gone. "You'll both know better than to fight again, won't you?" she said, patting their shoulders.

Between sniffles, they both answered, "Yes, Miss Endsley."

"Well, Blanche, Pearl, go on out to recess. Clara, you remain."

"Uh Oh," thought Clara. "Now what am I in for?"

"Come with me," said the principal and she led Clara out of the music room and into her office. On her desk sat the large red apple Clara had spotted earlier. Miss Endsley took the apple, bent down and gave it to Clara with a hug that was so quick Clara might have imagined it if it had not been for the look in Miss Endsley's eyes.

The principal drew herself up, straightened her back and shoulders, and said, "Remember, Clara, the rule is we do not fight to or from school." She gave Clara a pat that was close to a push. "Scoot now, go on out to recess." Clara took the apple, gave Miss Endsley a quick smile, and ran out the door. "Clara," Miss Endsley called, "Just eat the apple. No need to say anything to. . . " Clara was halfway down the hall before Miss Endsley finished her sentence but she heard very clearly what Miss Endsley told her.

She flew out the door onto the grass of the play-ground. "Blanche, Pearl," she yelled when she spotted them near the swings. "Look what I got. You got a paddling and didn't get nothin'. I got a paddling," she said, biting into the apple with a crunch, "and this juicy red apple."

Hide And Seek

'The Art of life is avoiding pain.'

Thomas Jefferson,
Letter to Mrs. Cosway, 1786

*I*t was morning, and in the small four-room brown house on Walnut street, the smell of burnt oatmeal hung heavy in the air. The family of nine children, minus one child—the oldest at sixteen had gone to see the world—plus one adult, were all jammed into the tiny house like the nursery rhyme's old woman who lived in a shoe. It was, for the most part, a comfortable fit. Though crowded, it was not cramped.

The middle child was crying. Clara did not want to go to school. She was trying every trick she knew to get her brother, Earl, to see it her way. After her Dad left the house for his work with the horses at the fairgrounds, she set out to soft soap or to bully Earl, whichever it took to bring him to her point of view. Earl was being stubborn today.

"Clara, you know what Dad told you the other day." Earl said. "Mom would want you to go to school. Now get ready! You're just not old enough or smart enough yet to quit." Earl's voice was firm.

"You're not the boss. Who do ya think you are, anyway?" yelled Clara. "Dad?"

"No. Mom," Earl said softly, more to himself than to Clara.

Clara, contrary to her natural inclination, resorted then to tears. But the tears did not move Earl an inch in the direction she wanted him to go. She had not expected such resistance. Even Mom had been easier to move.

"Mom," she thought, with an ache in her throat that threatened to shut off her breathing.

One day she was here. The next day she was gone. Nobody asked questions. Nobody offered answers. She pushed it from her mind, determined not to think or speak of it. To do so would make it true.

Knowing it was time to concede the morning's battle to Earl, Clara got ready, and she and her sister, Virginia, set out for Lincoln school.

They had rounded the corner at Division street when Clara caught sight of her brothers, Bill and Ralph, already by the railroad tracks almost halfway to school. She could see them standing too near the tracks, as usual, throwing rocks at the train. Old man Bennett, the watchman, was waving his arms like a goose flapping its wings, and motioning for them to move back. The sound of the train whistle cut through the air as the 8:45 Knickerbocker Special from Cleveland, Cincinnati, and Chicago gathered speed for the last leg of its journey to St. Louis.

Back home, Earl was cleaning up the dishes from breakfast and helping the little ones get dressed. He would be late for school as usual. How late depended on how soon one of his aunts could make it over to their house to look after the three youngest. Granny Golladay had offered to watch them at her house so Earl would not miss school, and for awhile Earl had loaded five-year old Holly, two-year old Mary Jane and baby Annabelle, into the little red, wooden wagon and pulled them the fourteen blocks to Granny's. But Granny's health had faded, and the rheumatiz now kept her in her rocking chair much of the time.

Earl's 6th grade teacher, Mrs. Rosebraugh and the principal, Miss Endsley had talked to him about missing so much school so he tried to explain the situation at home. "Dad needs me to help out around the house a little bit right now," he said.

Someone's got to be there to take care of the younger ones.

"I'm proud of you, Earl, for wanting to help your family," Miss Endsley had said. "But you can't be allowed to miss too much school." They had agreed to let him try, for awhile, to make up the work.

As Clara and Virginia neared the railroad, the last of the cars from the train were passing, and the trainman was waving from the platform of the red caboose. Virginia waved back but Clara stood still, listening to the sound of the whistle from the engine as it prepared to bank the slight curve west of town before it headed southwest toward St. Louis.

Clara shivered. "Cold, sis?" asked Virginia, pulling her small, thin sister close to her. She wondered if Clara had taken off her long underwear. Their Dad's rule, no matter how warm it got in May, was that long underwear was worn until the first official day of summer. There was no easy way to get around any of Dad's rules, so both girls had learned, after leaving and before returning home, to roll the scratchy long sleeves and legs of the woolen garment up under their outer clothing.

"It would be just like Clara to take hers off entirely, and wear those bloomers the welfare people brought over," thought Virginia, though all in the family old enough to comprehend, had been angry at the interference of the welfare people. Angriest of all had been Clara.

"Are you cold?" Virginia asked again, breaking into Clara's thoughts.

Clara turned her gaze away from the fast disappearing train and toward Virginia. "Naw. How could I be cold?" she answered. "It's the nicest day we've had all spring. It's just the sound of that ole train. . . gave me goose bumps like when I heard that screech owl last night."

"Scared?" ask Virginia, disbelief in her voice. She could not imagine her younger sister afraid of anything.

"No. . .not scared," Clara said, indignant." It's just. . .I hate that sound!" Clara's voice softened, "Lonely sort of. Like someone. . . " Her words faltered, "like some-one sayin' . . . good-by." She laughed quickly, then picked up a rock to throw at the caboose which was becoming a blur in the distance. "Bet I can hit that ole caboose," she said.

"Come on Clara Mae. We'll be late," said Virginia and she took off running. Clara stood for a second longer, watching till the caboose was completely out of sight. She caught up with Virginia and they made it to the edge of the school lot just as the school bell rang.

"Go on in, Virginia," said Clara. "I'll be there in just a few minutes."

"Now, Clara," warned Virginia, "Don't you go running off today."

"I won't," promised Clara, holding the fingers of her right hand crossed and hidden in the folds of her dress. The truth did not have to be told when you held king's x. Bill had told them that the other day and she would remind Virginia of it later if it hurt her feelings when she found out Clara had lied to her.

Clara was still standing just inside the school yard when Virginia looked back from the doorway. Seeing Clara still there made Virginia feel a little better, so she turned and walked to the fifth grade classroom she and her brother Bill shared. Moving so many times, and changing school so often, had put all of them back some and she and

Bill, with less than a year separating them in age, had ended up in the same classroom.

Clara was off and running, and at the bottom of Division Street hill as Virginia settled herself at her desk and opened her arithmetic book.

Clara ran fast all the way up the hill, past the hospital, then slowed her pace the next few blocks until she came to Polk Street. She turned west on Polk Street, still running and slightly out of breath. When she got close enough to Granny Golladay's little house, once white, now faded to gray, she could see Granny sitting outside on the porch in her rocking chair. A feeling of relief came over her, similar to the feeling she got when, tired of playing "Hide And Go Seek", the person who was "it" finally yelled out, "Olly, olly, ox—in free." Home base was in sight. Clara slowed down and walked the rest of the way.

Granny did not hear Clara come up to the porch, but the flutter of a shadow in the sunlight caused her to look up from her doze. "Well, Hi there, Clary," said Granny with a smile. "Ain't there no school today?"

"Nope, there ain't no school today, Grandma. So I come to visit you," said Clara, giving her a smile—and the answer they both wanted to hear.

Granny opened her arms, and Clara, though she was ten years old, ran to sit on her lap in the way she had when she was two. "You're my good ole grandma," Clara whispered, snuggling up and hiding in the softness that was Granny. She buried her face in the soap and cinnamon smells of Granny's apron.

Earl was walking up the stairs to his sixth grade class when he heard footsteps coming down which he knew belonged to Miss Endsley. Aunt Babe had come to the house this morning shortly after Virginia and Clara had left, so he was able to make it to school sooner than usual. "Earl," said Miss Endsley. "Where's Clara today? Is she sick?"

"Why, Miss Endsley," said Earl. She's here, ain't. . . .isn't she? She left for school with Virginia shortly before I did."

"Virginia's here. But Clara is not," replied Miss Endsley.

Earl stood, looking down at the scuff marks on his shoes. He did not speak for a few seconds, then he said, "I know where she is. I'll go get her."

"Earl," Miss Endsley's voice stopped him as he turned to walk back down the stairs, "Clara was on the third grade honor role last year. I'm sorry to see this happening." Earl did not know how to answer Miss Endsley, so he nodded in agreement, then turned to go find Clara.

Granny and Clara, enjoying the sunshine and the freedom of the brisk, spring day, had gone to check the fruit cellar for apples. "Fried apples will go good on a day like today," said Granny. Clara could already smell them cooking, could feel the tart sweet taste on her tongue. No one fried apples the way Granny did!

As they walked back around to the porch, they saw Earl coming toward them. "Why, Earl, what are you doin' here?" asked Granny. "Ain't you got no school today either?"

"I've got school, Grandma," said Earl. "And so does Clara. I've come to take her back."

"Durn it!" muttered Clara, moving closer to Granny. "Can't make me go!" She folded her arms and dug her heels into the soft dirt near the porch where the purple clematis would, in a month, be twining up the string Granny had tied there for it.

Earl laid his hand gently on her shoulder and his voice was soft but firm, "Come on now. You know you have to go to school."

It was the lack of anger in Earl, the sadness in his voice, that affected Clara the most. It would have been easier if he'd yelled at her, argued with her. She would have known how to battle back then. She would have known how to fight him. She was determined not to go back but she was at a loss over how to get her way without hurting Earl. Her small body telegraphed the message to his hand, still firmly grasping her shoulder, that she was not ready to give up.

"Clara?" he said, in a voice that was as close as he could come to pleading.

"Durn it! Why does he make it so hard for me. Can't he understand how it is now with me and school!" The words were not spoken aloud. Clara could not plead either.

"That stubborn family pride!" thought Granny Golladay watching the two locked in an battle that neither would really win. "It's as much a part of all those kids as the color of their eyes."

Clara grew impatient when she saw that Earl's resolve would allow him to stand there all day if he had to. Her anger came bubbling up and she squirmed under the hand on her shoulder, conjuring up from within, all kinds of names she could call to hurt him. In the experience of a ten-year old, living in a small town where everyone's ancestors were known back to Adam and where everybody watched what everybody else did, the worst possible thing was to be considered different. Clara had encountered that problem most of her life. She wasn't like any of the kids in her classroom; wasn't even like any of the eight other kids in her family. She had learned to live with it, had learned to use it to her advantage. But a few years back, she had chanced to come in contact with the worst way of being different, a more shameful way. It had made itself known to her when they lived in the house near the gas plant and the Calloways moved in next door. At least Clara's difference was largely on the inside, could be hidden part of the time; the Calloway's difference was on the outside, in plain sight of all the world.

Clara's jaw clenched and her heels dug deeper into the ground. She narrowed her eyes and her shoulders and drew herself inward. Through a mouth that seemed too narrow for the words to pass, she spat out, "Nigger, nigger!"

Earl shook his head slowly, his eyes showing weariness of battle, "I don't care what you call me, Clara. You're goin' to school."

With that, her heels loosened their grip on the earth. She turned and walked slowly, Earl's hold on her arm still firm, in the direction from which she had earlier, come running.

They reached the large brick school building far too soon for Clara's liking, and when they were inside, Earl removed his hand from her arm. Clara wouldn't look at him when he peered into her eyes in a plea for forgiveness, or at least compromise. "Now, stand right here, Clara. Don't move!" he said. "I'm going up to get Miss Endsley. Don't want to make you look the fool by dragging you into class."

As soon as Clara heard Earl's footsteps fade, she shot, like streak lightning, down the stairs to the basement and the girl's restroom. She went into one of the stalls, closed the door and climbed on the stool so she would not be visible in case the janitor or a teacher happened by.

It wasn't long before two sets of footsteps sounded in the hallway above. The precise clatter of

Miss Endsley's square heels hitting the marble and the flat sound of Earl's heavier step reached Clara's ears before their voices came floating down the stairs. "Earl, where's Clara?" asked Miss Endsley. "I thought you said she was here."

Disgust and aggravation caused Earl's voice to rise slightly. "She was supposed to wait right here. . . " he said, pointing to the spot where she had been standing when he left her. Both the principal and the boy sighed in defeat and resignation, for the time being, and turned and walked back up the stairs. Clara waited until she could hear no voices, no footsteps, then slipped from her hiding place. Her exit out of the building was swift. When she got to the edge of the school yard, she repeated her early morning flight. She was slightly out of breath as she reached Polk Street, so she slowed down until, once more, she caught sight of Granny's little gray house and of Granny on the front porch sitting in her rocking chair.

As Clara drew near the front porch, Granny looked up and smiled. "Well, hi Clary," she said. "Ain't there no school today?"

"Nope. There ain't no school today, Grandma. So I come to visit you," said Clara, giving her a smile—and the answer they both wanted to hear.

The Sparrow & the Hawk

*T*here was no doubt about it. They were closely related, brother and sister most likely—the man and the woman sitting at the kitchen table. Both had hair as black as Brazil, Indiana coal with very little gray. And both had the kind of olive-brown skin people envy because it retains its firmness longer; seems to age slower. It was true, neither face showed the years much. The most visible wrinkles on the face of the woman were around the eyes, laugh lines they're usually called. Most likely they'd been there since she was a child, only now they'd deepened.

She was a woman who laughed easily; she had always been able to find something to laugh about. There were no laugh lines on the face of the man. He was not given to laughing much. Those who had known him most of his life might have described him as an easy-going kind of man who cared about kids and dogs and those on the down-under side of life. Oh, he would bluster once in awhile and liked to argue; would probably say black if you said white just to get things going. But really, he was more of a worrier than a warrior. Now his sister Clara, who sat here beside him at the table. . . she was the one who could be called the battler of the family. In fact, she came into this world battling as she drew her first breath.

Clara leaned over to take a cigarette from the pack, got one for her brother and pushed the ashtray within his reach and slightly out of hers, making it easier for him, more difficult for herself.

"Damn things!" Earl said. "Tried to give them up. Stopped for awhile, too. But here I am again. . . ."

Clara laughed to show she understood. But she said, "Ah, you worry to much, Earl, You're pushin' eighty now. Couldn't have hurt you much. Enjoy 'em!"

"Be eighty this November," Earl said, picking up on only one of her remarks. "Been a short trip, hasn't it? Been a short trip." Earl gazed off toward the hollyhocks growing in the alley outside his open kitchen door. His eyes saw neither those hollyhocks nor that door; saw instead hollyhocks growing beside another kitchen door in another time. He shook his head, a smile on his face at the memory, fresh and crisp as the leaf lettuce he'd picked from his small garden only that morning.

"Whatcha' thinkin' about, Earl?" asked Clara, watching his eyes, his half-sad smile.

"Oh," he sighed. "Mom, Dad. . . when we were kids."

They sat in silence for a minute, both of them deep in their own thoughts. "Been thinking about it some myself lately," admitted Clara, nodding her head. 'Tough ole' times. Survived though, didn't we!" She laughed then, a light silvery laugh.

Earl caught his breath, closed his eyes at the sound of her laugh. He was thirteen years old again and it was his mother laughing.

Clara's laughter trailed off. Old pain refused to be done away with so easily this time. Caught up in her own visions of the past, she did not notice Earl's silence. "We're good people," she bristled and her voice changed from the quiescent musing of a minute before to a strident battle readiness. Her thin frame rose slightly from the wooden chair and her fists clenched on the table. "Better not anybody say any different!"

"She's still battling," Earl thought. He smiled and his face showed the affection and indulgence and acceptance he felt for this sister who was as different from him as a cockle-burr from a cotton ball.

Earl leaned in toward Clara and his face grew serious. "I think about those days a lot. Always have. Now brother Ray, he was of another mind. He'd say to me, "Earl, why do you care? Just go on. Forget about it. It's not between us. We can't solve other people's problems. " There was a touch of hurt and bewilderment in the tone of Earl's voice that hung on in the silence that followed.

He went on, "I never felt the way Ray did. I always looked for answers to things. Never found them though," he admitted, shaking his head. "Not really."

What had they to show for it, he suddenly thought, seeing, for a change, the whole puzzle instead of the individual pieces. For all his worrying and for all Clara's battling, the earth had gone right on spinning; right on sailing around the sun. He rubbed his eyes as if to rub away the unwelcome vision. "It all goes 'round and 'round in my mind, " he said, still rubbing his eyes. "Lately those days seem more crystal clear to me, more real than all the years after. A lot more real than today!"

Clara looked straight at her brother. "Guess I didn't much want to think about it. Not then. Guess I was too busy makin' things happen. Don't know why it is just lately. . . " She twisted around in the chair, peered over at the sink to satisfy herself that there were no dishes that needed washing. Seeing none, Clara turned her attention to the table and began straightening up the few items that lay there. She refolded the morning newspaper and slid it under her purse and smoothed out the wrinkles of the red paisley headscarf that lay on top of the purse. "Just lately," she repeated, her thin fingers still working at the wrinkles of her scarf, "I've wondered 'bout some things."

Earl's eyebrows raised slightly in surprised. This was a different Clara! He had missed altogether her earlier admission that she was, lately, reflecting on the past. He had never been a listener and the years had given greater license to his habit of selectively isolating one word in a conversation to springboard himself back into his own thoughts.

Not comfortable with anything that felt like change, he turned his thoughts quickly back to the Clara he had always known. *He* was the one who looked back and measured every step he had taken. Now Clara. . . "You. . . now you were a wild one, Clara!" His smile softened his words and his words returned them safely to old and familiar ground.

"Most people would tell you I still am." Clara said with a grin. "Didn't change much over the years, did I ? But I've been wonderin'. . .don't remember things good as you do, Earl. You were always around takin' care of things, the old sluggy-go dependable one. Dad relied on you a lot after Mom left."

Earl smiled at her choice of words. . .'sluggy-go dependable one'. It was what his older brother had always said about him. Exact words, in fact. The words fit like the well-tailored suit he had never owned. But then he'd had years of wearing those words, years to grow accustomed to their fit. He turned his attention to Clara again. "You were busy makin' things happen alright. Seemed to do that from the minute you arrived. Well, can't say I actually saw you the minute you arrived but it wasn't too long after. . . "

Clara got up, took the blackened aluminum coffee pot, which was always kept hot and filled, from the back burner of the white enameled stove. She poured the steaming, mud-black coffee into both their cups, then sat down again. "Where were we living when I was born," she asked? "I never did hear anybody say. Never thought to ask before."

"In an old two-story brick house that sat at the corner of Division and State Streets," said Earl. "Where Gilman's little old store building sits now. I remember Mom saying we lived in about three different places that year. But that's where we were living in November when you were born. You know, Clara, I was reading the other day about a tribe of people somewhere in Ethiopia . . . village called Issere. Those people name their kids according to what's happenin' on the day the child is born. If that had been the custom here in the midwest in 1913, Mom and Dad would of probably named you 'Stormy' or 'Thunder'." He paused, contemplating, "Maybe they know something, those Ethiopians. The name 'Thunder' would have fit you a whole lot better than the name Clara."

"I agree with you." said Clara, musing. "'Stormy' or 'Thunder' might fit me better than Clara. But I always liked the name Clara."

"Named for Mom's sister," said Earl. "You were little Clara. She was big Clara. 'Course, most everybody called her Clede, 'cept you. You just called her Aunt Clara." He solemnly passed on the information as if it were news rather than the same words she had heard over and over since she was old enough to listen.

"Aunt Clara was the pretty sister, I guess" said Clara. Perhaps it was a family trait, this pouncing on words and ignoring sentences. Perhaps only a human trait. She jumped up quickly from the chair. "Got any sweets, Earl," she asked? He pointed toward the cupboard, and she walked over, opened the doors, and rummaged around. She came back to the table with a package of chocolate donuts in her hand. "Not like when Elma was alive, is it? Just this ole store-bought stuff." She reached over and patted his hand, then took out a donut and bit into it. "I always could eat anything I wanted and never gain an ounce," she said with a laugh. After a few bites, she laid the donut down. She sat without moving, looking down at her cup. "Granny Golladay always called me Clary, remember? I can hear her voice yet, the way she said it. 'Clary'! Like a song that starts low and rises quickly." She sat looking off, repeating the sound. "'Clary'. . . "

"Granny was there the night you were born." said Earl. "I was only four, but I'll never forget it. Ray was five. Virginia was three, and Bill was just a baby. Don't think he was even walking yet."

Clara pushed the donut package toward Earl. He took one and laid it down in front of him in an absentminded way; his eyes looking, but not seeing, in the same way he had earlier looked out toward the hollyhocks.

"What I remember most about the day you were born," Earl began, " was the weather." It was a fierce day, hot and stormy, not cool like you'd expect for November. And rain! I'd been told the story of Noah's ark when Aunt Ann had taken Ray and me to Sunday school, and I kept worryin' and thinkin' we'd better hurry and start buildin' a boat.

108

I expect it would have been the best way to get around town that day. Horse and buggy couldn't. And nobody but a few of the rich or adventuresome had autos. The rain and the flooding wasn't the worst of it, though. The wind and lightning was what had people running for shelter.

I remember bein' scared and trying to stay close to Mom. I don't know which scared me most, the storm or the way Mom was actin'. I could tell something was wrong with her, the way she kept drawing her breath in and folding her arms around her stomach. But she never stopped for long. Kept on working around the house, singing songs to us, trying to keep our minds off the storm. Probably, at the same time, trying to keep her mind off what I later realized, were labor pains.

She had just gotten the front room floor scrubbed—had pushed us kids off into the kitchen while it was drying. You know how she was always so ticky about her house, Clara. Had to keep the floors clean enough to eat off of. She kept calling into the kitchen reminding us to stay away from the windows because of all that lightning. She could have saved her breath because all three of us kids were jumping every time the thunder crashed. We had no curiosity at all about what was accompanying the booming noise.

In the middle of a crash that rattled the windows and every dish in the kitchen, we heard Mom cry out. "Ray! Earl!" she yelled. "Run get me some newspapers." Ray and I were making a train out of the kitchen chairs and I was lifting Virginia, trying to put her into the caboose. When I heard Mom's cry, I dropped Virginia, knocking the chair over on top of her. Ray and I looked at each other with bewilderment. Wasn't like Mom to stop and read newspapers in the middle of her cleanin'. Usually nothin' got in the way of that, not even us.

"Quick now! " she yelled again. And we could hear the impatience in her voice. We ran to where the newspapers were kept stacked near the coal bucket. When we got to the front room, Mom was standing behind the old Warm Morning stove in a puddle of water. "Help me now," she said in the impatient voice she had used earlier. "Help me spread the newspapers to soak up the water. No! Not like that Earl!" she snapped. "Spread them thicker! Ray, get me the alarm clock Dad keeps by the side of the bed." She turned to me again. "Virginia's crying," she said as if I couldn't hear for myself. "Go help her."

I ran to get Virginia untangled from the kitchen chair. She wasn't hurt, just mad at being left in there by herself. When Virginia and I got back to the front room, Ray was there with the clock. "Set it on the library table, Ray, and face it toward me." Mom said.

Ray did as he was told and then we kids stood watching Mom—and she stood watching the clock. I couldn't have put it into words way back then, but I think that's the first time I ever felt abandoned. It seemed as if our Mother had disappeared and in her place, standing behind that stove and wearing her clothes, was a stranger.

We knew Dad was due home at noon for lunch but well before 12:00, Dad came in the back door. He was wet and bedraggled, his red hair springing up in whispy curls around his cap. For once, he was not whistlin' his way into the house. "It's bad out there," he said. "Told them at the gas plant I had to run home and check on you, Jennie. See how you and the kids were doing." He took a look at Mom, then at us kids and back again at Mom.

"George," Mom said, without taking her eyes off the clock. She was standing absolutely still on the newspapers behind the stove.

He said, "I'll get the neighbor boy to go for Granny Golladay," and Dad turned and ran back out into the storm. In no time at all, he was back. "Come on Jennie," he said, gently leading Mom into the bedroom. Ray, Virginia and I were close on their heels and in the bedroom with them before Mom had settled under the covers. "Come on kids," Dad said. "Help me in the kitchen." As soon as Dad got the fire stoked up in the cook stove and got a big pan of water boiling, he told Mom he thought he'd better send for Doc Craig.

He had gone out the back door to find someone to go for the doctor when Granny Golladay arrived. The wind blew her and the driving rain in the front door, getting Mom's clean floor all wet again. Behind her, we could see the lightning splitting the sky and hear the thunder crashing. Aunt Babe was with her and neither had a dry spot on them.

I don't know how in the world they made it all the way there from out on Polk Street in that weather. They had no horse and buggy so I guess they walked. But I don't know for sure. I do know they headed straight for the bedroom and taking one look at Mom, Aunt Babe remarked, "We'd better get the kids over to the neighbor's right away." I didn't want to leave, huddled down under the bed thinking to hide but Aunt Babe saw me and wouldn't put up with no shenanigans. "No back talk now," she told me when I protested loudly. She bundled us up best she could against the wet and took us next door to wait out your arrival.

I guess Doc Craig got there soon after we left. Dad met him up on the square several years later, and you know, Dad said Doc was still talking and shaking his head about that night. First of all, he liked to never made it to our house, and it wasn't all that long a distance either, from his house on Harrison Street to where we were living there on State. I guess he finally gave up trying to hitch the horse to the buggy; instead rode his horse through the streets, belly deep in water part of the time, with the wind blowing him back almost every step of the way. I guess he had quite a time! But Doc maintained later that traveling in that storm was a picnic social compared to what he encountered in the bedroom inside the old brick house."

Earl stopped and lit another cigarette. "Some say that people come into this world already a lot of what they're going to be," Earl went on. "Kicking and squalling or smiling and cooing. I guess you know, Clara Mae, which way you entered the world. Your yell was so ear-splitting that Doc Craig told Dad he wore cotton in his ears for weeks after.

By the time Granny Golladay came over to fetch us, the storm had abated outside and inside the old brick house, and they had you all cleaned up and looking pretty civilized. But we knew from the aftermath, that we had ourselves a warrior.

We marched single-file through the kitchen door, with Ray leading the way, me next, and then Virginia. Granny was last, carrying the sleeping Bill. As we came through the door, we heard, well before we saw, Dad and this little bitty, black-haired, red-skinned baby girl. He had you cradled in his arms, waltzing around on that old, uneven, wooden kitchen floor. Dad was singing to you,

Clara, in the clear tenor voice that had, one time or another, calmed us all.

My gal, she's a high-born lady.
She's dark, but not too shady.
Feathered like a peacock, and just as gay[2]

You were wiggling and squirming in his arms. But you were quiet. We all stopped dead-still just inside the door, even Granny, burdened as she was with Bill. We didn't move; we were mesmerized by the sight, but more so by the sound. Oh, it's not as if we were hearing Dad singing for the first time. Heaven knows, it was as much a part of our lives as breathing and the stick-to-your-ribs oatmeal he made us eat every morning for breakfast. Even then, the sound of his music held us spellbound. We never tired of it. It was a splash of bright yellow in our gray-brown world.

Dad had just gotten to the part in the song we always liked best. You remember the part that goes,"

Well, there's Miss Linolia Davis,
and there's Miss Glenolia Brown,
and there's Miss Joanna Beasley
all dressed up in red.
I just hugged her and I kissed her
and then she said,
"Man, oh man, do not let me fall.
If I can't have you, I'll have no man at all.
There'll be a hot time in the old town tonight.

2

Fagan, Barney. (1896). My Gal, She's a High Born Lady.

Dad had glimpsed us standin' there watchin' and listen' but he paid us no mind. That dance was your's, Clara, and was not over 'til he decided it was over.

Just then we heard Mom's laugh from the bedroom, "George! What a song to sing to a new-born babe." Reassured by the calm matter-of-factness of her voice after the storm-filled hours spent apart, Ray and I raced to the bedroom to see for ourselves that Mom was still Mom.

Virginia ran over to where Dad and you were still dancing and as I looked back, I saw that he, in one graceful move had bent his long, lanky frame down and swooped her up. "May I have this dance," he said to Virginia. As he whirled both of you around we heard him say to you, "Clara Mae, meet your big sister, Amy Virginia."

Clara had sat without moving the whole time Earl was telling the story. "You know, we kids were always Dad's best audience."

"I guess his only audience unless you count all the thoroughbreds he doctored and trained at the fairgrounds, and the stables around Charleston," reflected Earl.

"Or," Clara quickly added, " those men Mom called his cronies down at the Silver Moon or McGurty's Tavern on Monroe Street. Remember how she used to send us down on Fridays to get his paycheck in case he decided to head for Whiskey Row before he headed for home? We'd usually find him there on one of the street corners singing with his friends.

"I'd give anything, just this minute, to hear him again, " said Earl. "*By the light of the Silvery Moon*," he began singing, then humming, when the words slipped from his grasp.

Clara began humming along with him, then she, too, sang a few lines of the song. "Sometimes we wouldn't catch him early enough," she reminded Earl.

"They'd really get to singing good then, he and his friends, after some of that oil of forgetfulness had been flowin' through their veins a few hours. But Dad didn't have to be drinkin' to sing. Wasn't he something though, Clara? Forever singin', whistlin', yodelin', dancin'? He could do a little bit of everything, couldn't he? Even draw. Boy could he draw! Now that's where you got your drawin' talent, Clara. Me, I can't even draw a stick. Can't carry a song in a suitcase either, though it never kept me from tryin'. But you. . . you took after Dad in a lot of ways. "

"Guess so. Always thought I'd find a man like that to marry. Six times, or was it seven, thought I had." laughed Clara. "Oh, I loved Dad, but still I was my Momma's girl."

"Mom had a lot to put up with, that's for sure." said Earl. "He came up that sidewalk singin' *Sweet Adeline* more often than I want to remember."

Clara laughed again. "I'd almost forgotten. That's the song that always told Mom—told all of us—Dad had lifted a few too many. I'll never forget one night when we lived over by the gas plant, and Dixie Dora lived right across the street. Dad came home late one night, singin' *Sweet Adeline* and Mom tried to quiet him. " George, lower your voice, " she whispered. " If I lived around here I'd call the police on you for disturbing the peace."

"I recall that night," said Earl, "Remember what Dad said then? Said, "Why, Jane, you do live around here.""

"Mom didn't like that much, did she?" Clara said. "Then Dad got out the broom and started, of all things, to sweep off the front sidewalk and he never could, when he had a broom in his hand, resist doing his dance and broom twirling routine could he?"

They both smiled. . . remembering.

Earl, who had been content to sit and let Clara wait on him earlier, now got up from the kitchen chair with the vigor of a much younger man. He got the broom from its corner by the pantry, and began twirling it and dancing. "Now how did he do that, Clara? It was just an old kitchen broom, not balanced at all like a baton would be, and he would lift it up and twirl it over his head," Earl said, demonstrating, "and down between his legs."

Breathing hard, he leaned the broom against the table and sat back down. "Just an old kitchen broom," he said between gasps for air, " and Dad could make magic with it."

"Magic," Clara agreed, nodding. "Dixie Dora sure loved his magic. That night when Dad started sweepin' off the front sidewalk and singin' and dancin', I was watchin' from the bedroom window and laughin' to myself. Then I heard ole Dixie clap her hands and yell out from her porch swing. I started to get mad 'cause I thought she was makin' fun of him. But then, ole Dixie called out, "George, you ought to be with that vaudeville troupe that was up at the opera house last week. You'd put all of 'em to shame. Let's hear that song; see that dance one more time!" And she started clappin' again. Just short of a standin' ovation, she was givin' him."

"Boy! Did Mom ever get mad!" Clara continued. "She was mutterin' under her breath, "Old sorgum-sweet hussy. Wish she'd just mind her own business," loud enough for Dad to hear but not loud enough to carry across the street. Of course, Dad tried to calm her down like he always did, "Now, Jennie," he said, putting his arm around her.

Mom just turned on her heels and headed back toward the house still muttering, "Nothin' but a grass widow, that woman is! Sits there mindin' everyone's business but her own. Waitin' for a man that isn't ever gonna marry her."

You know Earl, Dixie is the one that wanted us to name Holly that crazy name, Holly Orville E. Ripley Jackson Clark Easter—after her boy-friend. The one that never did marry her. "

"Mom didn't want any help namin' her babies," said Earl. "Not even promises of the finest go-cart in town could get Mom to go along with Dixie on that name. Mom was pretty stubborn in her own way—sometimes."

Earl picked up the donut beside his coffee cup and began, unconsciously, breaking it into small pieces. "What it was though, the main problem. . . " His words became almost inaudible. He cleared his throat. "What it was, I think, with Mom. . . and Dad. . . is that. . .what one loved, the other one hated and what one hated, the other one loved. Just couldn't agree."

"Earl, I've gotta' go," said Clara, gathering up her purse and scarf. "Nobody knows where I am." She squinched her face and shoulders up and giggled, deepening the laugh lines around her eyes. "I've run away from home again!"

Earl followed her out onto the porch. Clara gave him a hug and a kiss and walked down the steps. She stopped at the bottom and turned to him and said, "It was because of Aunt Clara. She told Mom the only way she would ever have a life of her own was to get away from all us kids and Dad."

Noises from above caused them to look up. High in the sky, above the fence row of trees, next to the cornfield, to the east of Earl's house, a red-tailed hawk flew in circles, seemingly ignoring the brown sparrow that hovered above him. The tiny warrior swooped down time and again, landing upon the back of the hawk, pecking and scolding him, raining attack on the larger bird with all the fury possible in its small body.

Earl shaded his eyes against the bright sunlight as he and Clara kept their eyes fastened on the lopsided battle. The hawk continued to sail around in the heavens, as if the sparrow did not exist, oblivious to the small bird's instinctive and furious battle to survive and to protect its own.

This is the Cat Bowl Story
(It Goes With the Cat Bowl)

"Anything that can go wrong, will go wrong."

Murphy's Third Law

▶ Cat Bowl—A haunting cat design with a native western image is glazed on our handmade ceramic bowl. This fascinating vessel from North Eagle Pottery of California is an unusual planter and an inspiring container for unique dried plant materials. 7½" × 7½"

Cat Bowl, #447, $65.00

*D*ear Key and Uwe,

From the moment I saw it, I knew it was made for you. "That Cat Bowl belongs to Key and Uwe," I thought. My search for the perfect wedding gift for the two of you was over. I could picture the blue and white hand-made, earthenware bowl, with a green sprengeri fern growing gracefully up and over the edges, the mystical blue cat on the side of the bowl peeking out through the feathery fronds. It would look perfect sitting in your home among all your other tropical vegetation.

When we visited you in Texas last February, I was impressed by the way your plants grew and flourished under your green thumbs. However, I couldn't help but notice that the plants reflected your two previously separate lives; some of them 'his' plants and some of them 'hers'. What better way to symbolize the beginning of your married life together than an 'ours' plant. And what better home for the 'ours' plant than a mystical blue and white Cat Bowl. I was sure, too, that another cat would be welcomed into your family. Even a blue one.

I marked page ten in the *Faith Mountain Catalog Company* where I had seen the pot and the description of the Cat Bowl but before I could place the order, I needed to figure out how to get it to you in Texas since we, as you know, would be unable to make it to the wedding. I then went to the local flower shop where only the very best plants are grown and asked the young man working there if he thought it would be possible to send a very fragile sprengeri fern in a very breakable Cat Bowl to Dallas, Texas.

"Can't be done," the young man said, patting the soil around the red geranium he was potting.

I could see I didn't have his full attention. I decided to appeal to his sense of romance and challenge. So I began to tell him about the forthcoming marriage of a seven-foot, two-inch German immigrant who, several years ago, came to play basketball at a high school near by, then went on to play at Indiana University, and had now attained what most young, and old, boys dream of—a chance to play pro. And I talked of the bride-to-be, a six-foot Texas beauty whose namesake ancestor's anthem was sung before just about every sporting event in America.

I did not stop there. I went on to talk about the benefits of green growing things on planet Earth, the art of choosing the right gift, the importance of good beginnings, mystical Cat Bowls, and fate. Sometimes it is possible to carry people along on the waves of enthusiasm. Or is it talking fast and persistence that works? Soon the young man was saying, "I think it's a great idea. Bring me your Cat Bowl and I'll plant a nice fern in it; help you get it ready to mail. I don't really see a problem. Sure we can do it!"

So now I had to get the Cat Bowl. All Cat Bowls begin life in the *North Eagle Pottery Shop* in California and from there they go to a village in Virginia called Sperryville where the *Faith Mountain Catalog Company* oversees their distribution.

I phoned *Faith Mountain* and asked if they would, very carefully, mail me a Cat Bowl.

When it arrived a week later, I took it to the flower shop but the easy-to-convince, eager-to-help young man was not there. In his place was a friendly but pessimistic gray-haired lady. "Oh, honey," she said. "It just can't be done! There is no way your Cat Bowl and our fern would make it to Texas in one piece. Why the stories I could tell you!" She shut her eyes and shuddered as if to block out visions of dead and mangled plants that had been delivered to their doorstep by UPS and by the United States postal service. "Don't even think about it! It can't be done."

Something told me right away she could not be swayed. Certain people are oblivious to matters of fate. But the Cat Bowl belonged to you and, one way or another, you would have it. "Will you plant the fern in the bowl?" I asked with what I hoped was polite determination. There was nothing left to do but follow the advice of Napoleon I who was well acquainted with the burden of destiny, and who said something like, "If you want something done, well do it yourself."

I made my way home with your Cat Bowl, the delicate sprengeri cascading over the bowl in just the way I had envisioned. I sat it in our living room and looked at it, and dragged out box after box, and thought about how best to pack it. The longer I looked, the stronger I doubted. Then it came to me. There's more than one way to send a cat. I would keep THIS Cat Bowl (I had grown fond of it by now anyway). I would call my niece Vickie, who also lives in Dallas, explain the situation and ask her if I could have a Cat Bowl (your's for sure, this time) sent to her from Sperryville; have her take the bowl to her florist where they would plant the sprengeri fern, then deliver it to you along with a card which I would mail to Vickie in time for delivery. Several phone calls and several notes later it was all set. By the 8th of June, at the very latest, you would be the proud owners of a fantastic Cat Bowl. You would have time before the pre-wedding rush to enjoy it; ample time to contemplate its beauty and symbolism.

On Friday, June 10th, the phone rang and it was you, Uwe. "Oh, how nice," I thought, slight triumph tinged with great relief. "Key and Uwe have finally received their Cat Bowl. They are calling to tell us how much they like it." I waited for you to mention it. And waited. And waited. When you didn't, I was puzzled. "Do they hate it?" I wondered. "Or. . .Is it possible they didn't receive it?" After I hung up, (not a word had been spoken about the Cat Bowl), I called Vickie to make sure it had been delivered. Vickie was not home and it wasn't until later that night she returned my call.

"Hi Aunt Nancy," she began, minus her usual enthusiasm. There was an unnatural silence. And I waited.

Vickie broke the silence, "I have something to tell you." Again silence. Again I waited. "It's about the Cat Bowl," she began again and this time her words came spilling out. "It arrived on Tuesday, the 7th. Arrived in perfect shape. You were right! It's beautiful. I did as we'd planned. Took it to the florist where I told you I trust them to do good work."

Vickie hesitated again, in contrast to her normal spontaneity, then went on, "They had the right type fern, the sprengeri. One problem but nothing major. The only sprengeri they had was way too large; had to be broken up. It'd take a little more time but the manager assured me they could get it delivered by the 9th. Oh yes, and I remembered to give them the card. The one you mailed me for Key and Uwe."

Vickie, being Vickie, gave them one further instruction. She told them to call her when the fern was planted in the bowl so she could go by and take a picture of it for me.

At this point in the story I breathed easier. Vickie went on with her story. "On the 9th, the shop called to say the Cat Bowl was ready so I went by and took photos of it. It looked great, Aunt Nancy. You would have been pleased. Then I asked them to call me when delivery had been made so I could let you know."

The next day, Friday, was a busy day for Vickie and it wasn't until evening that she realized the expected call from the florist had never come.

"Ah ha!" I thought. "The old good-news-bad-news tactic. Now it comes. . .the part about the Cat Bowl breaking. I'll bet the delivery man. . . !"

But I was wrong. It was not as simple as that. Nothing ever is. This is the story the florist told Vickie; this is the story Vickie told me; this is the story I now tell you.

The delivery man set off that afternoon to make his deliveries, and tucked safely inside the van full of flowers and plants was your Cat Bowl with the sprengeri fern. The driver stopped to make a delivery and left the motor of the van running while he crawled into the back to look for the flowers he was to leave at that address. At that very moment, an armed robber, fleeing pursuit by the police, saw opportunity in the shape of a green and white florist van, the door open and the motor running. The robber jumped in behind the wheel and took off at great speed. Nobody knows exactly what happened next but at some point during the next four hours, the delivery man was drugged.

"Dragged?" I asked.

"No, drugged," Vickie repeated. "And then thrown out of the van."

The drugged delivery man was found lying unconscious on a side street in Dallas far from the first intended delivery. The Dallas police theory was that the robber was using the florist van only as a get-away car; that it would be found later, its cargo intact. When this happened, they would notify the florist, the florist would notify Vickie, Vickie would notify me, and we would advance from there.

Two days later, Sunday, the van was found abandoned on a country road somewhere outside Dallas. The robber must have liked the Cat Bowl. It was gone, along with everything else. The only thing left behind was the card lying in the dusty road alongside the van, smudges of dirt and the names Key and Uwe on the outside of the envelope.

For the third time, I called *Faith Mountain Catalog Company* in Sperryville, Virginia. For the third time, I ordered a Cat Bowl. By this time, according to Vickie, and the manager of the flower shop, somewhere in your apartment in Dallas, should be *Blue and White Handmade, Earthenware Cat Bowl Number Three*, the green sprengeri fern growing gracefully up and over the edges, the mystical blue cat on the side of the bowl, peeking out through the feathery fronds; just as was intended from the beginning.

Every time I walk into our living room or water the fern growing green and lush in *Cat Bowl Number One*, I think of you and your *Cat Bowl Number Three*. And I can't help but wonder about *Cat Bowl Number Two*. Did it survive and does it now grace some unknown thief's abode? Does someone shower, with love and with water, the fern so carefully chosen, so carefully planted? Does the plant thrive, sending a jungle of green over the side of the bowl for the mystical blue cat to peek through? Or, does the blue cat sit, covered with dust, alone and forgotten, in some corner, the fern inside dry and withered from neglect? Most of all, I wonder: does its present owner ever sense that, by crook and by chance, his life became intertwined with the three lives of a Cat Bowl?

Love and BestWishes,

Nancy

P. S. On your silver anniversary, I think I'll send money.

Index

Note

It is unusual to offer an index in a book of short stories. However, because these stories are about real people and real events, most of the names, places and dates are actual. For those who appreciate the details of common-place history, we offer some assistance.

Dates

A

B

Gerine v
Holly (Holly Orville
E. Ripley Jackson
Clark Easter) v,
66—68, 72, 76, 92,
117
Jane Golladay Easter
Slough (Also
Jennie—Earl's
Mother or Mom)
65, 68, 71, 73, 74,
84, 91, 104, 106,
107, 109—117
Joshua v
Luke 50
Mary Jane v, 68, 70,
72, 75, 92, 115
Ray v, 75, 76, 113,
116, 117, 118, 121,
123
Sara v
Virginia (Amy
Virginia) 68—76,
83, 84, 92—96,
108—114
Eastern Illinois
University
(Normal School) 33
Old Main 33
Eastin
Captain John
Michael 24, 25, 40
Jennie K. Reed 24,
40
Major Charles 40
Editor 41
Elks building 29, 30, 36,
37
Ellington 25

Embarras River 53, 56,
60
Endsley, Antha
Euphemia 67, 81—
88, 92—99
Ethiopia, Issere 107

F

Face, Elroy 50
Fairgrounds 27, 86, 91,
114
*Faith Mountain Catalog
Company* ii, 121,
122, 123, 126
Farmer 40, 41, 85
Farmer's Almanac 53
Feller, Bobby 50
Ferguson, Mrs. Dr.
(Susan Morton) 22,
23
Fifth Grade 94
Ford, Whitey 50
Fox, Nellie 49
France
Hotel De France 3
Paris 3
Sun King's Palace 3
Versailles 3
Fringe tree 36
Frock coat 18
Funeral dirge 69, 70

G

Gambling 25
Garner, Sue Ellen vi
Gas plant 66, 71, 76, 98,
110

I

Illinois v, ix, 12, 16, 19,
21, 22, 31, 33, 35,
6, 41, 47, 53, 55, 143
Ashmore Township
38
Champaign 33
Charleston vi., ix,
14, 20, 24, 28, 29,
31, 32, 35, 37, 38—
43, 53, 55, 57—60,
114, 143
Chicago 23, 33, 38,
47, 92
Coles County 31, 32,
33, 39, 40, 53, 143
Embarras
Grand Prairie 20
Grandview 36
Mattoon 33
Paris 36
Rardin 53, 55, 57, 58
Riley Creek 32
Shelbyville 12
Springfield 55
Wabash 12, 13, 19,
20, 25, 33
Illinois state legislature
33
Indian 38, 58
Indian encampments 38
Indiana
Brazil 103
Indianapolis 33
Terre Haute 12, 13
Indiana poet (James
Whitcomb Riley) 32
Indiana University 122
Irish jig 69

J

Jefferson, Thomas 36,
89
Jones, Babe Golladay
(See Golladay)

K

Kaline, Al 50
Ka-Ne-Kuk 38
Kaskaskias 38
Kentucky 22, 25, 33, 40
Lexington 40
first white male child
40
Kentucky blue grass 33
Kickapoos 38
Kline, Ronnie 50
Knickerbocker Special
92
Knock,
Emma 51—-61
Home (See
Golladay)
John 53—56
Mary (See Golladay)
Knock's Holler 5—56,
59
Knock's tenant farms 58
Kucks, Johnny 50
Kuenn, Harvey 50

L

Ladd, Marta 143
Lard 66, 74
Latin 22

Q

Queen Anne House 26, 28, 37, 42
Queen Bees 41

R

Reasor,
Marie Sayre Gramesly (See Gramesly)
Record's Tile and Brick Factory 67
Revolutionary War 35
Reynolds, Allie 50
Rhodes, Dusty 50
Rigby, Billy 27, 33
Riley,
James 33
James Whitcomb 32
Rizzuto, Phil 50
Robber 125, 126 (thief)
Roe, Preacher 50
Rosebraugh, Margaret 81, 82, 92, 98
Roses (Yellow Rose or Rosa Harisonii) 23, 24, 75, 81
Ruth, Babe 47

S

Sain, Johnny 50
Saltbox 53, 60
Sand cherry 36
Sandburg, Carl 9
Sauer, Hank 50
School

Eastern Illinois University (Normal) (See Eastern Illinois University) 35
High School v, 122
Lincoln (See Lincoln School)
Sunday 108
Teachers v
Sconce, Thomas 39
Scott, Frank ii
Sedimentary rock 34
Senior Citizens 37
Shafer, Matty 65
Shantz, Bobby 50
Shick,
Andrew 43, 143
April Stout v, 143
Brittany 30, 43, 143
Daniel 43, 143
David (Dave) v, 143
DeAnne (Brittany's Mother) 30
Lonnie v, 143
Mitchell v, 143
Ryan 45, 143
Shoe Factory 70
Shriver (Mary Jane Easter) v
Silver maples 30, 35
Silver Moon Saloon 114
Simpson, Suitcase 50
Slaughter, Enos 50
Slaves 17
Sluggy-go 106
Smyser, Della 4, 5, 6
Snyder, Sheryl 43
Soap (See Home-made Soap)
Solitary life 57

139

140

Warrior 38, 103, 112,
    118
Washington 84
Washpan 66, 68, 72
Washtub 68, 73
Welfare 84, 87, 93
Whiskey 71
Whiskey Row 114
White Art Moderne
    House 36, 37
White Bungalow 36, 37,
    42
White Sox 47
Whiteside, Dr. Wesley
    vi
Wild Flowers 57
Wilhelm, Hoyt 50
Williams, Teddy (Ted)
    50
Wilson, C. E. 33
Wingate, Louise
    (Norfolk) 40
Woodson,
    James 28, 42
    Margaret 28, 42
World (Reference to) 5,
    25, 26, 36, 48, 55,
    59, 60, 67, 76, 98,
    103, 111, 112, 113
World Series 48
Wynn, Early 50

Y

Yankee 18, 47, 48
Yankee Stadium 48

About the Author

Nancy Easter Shick is the mother of three: April, Mitchell and Lonnie and the grandmother of eight: Katie, Kirstin, Alexandra, Brittany, Ryan, Andrew, Daniel and, of course, Hank. She and her husband Dave own and operate Best Construction Company in Charleston, Illinois. This is Nancy's third book. The first, The History of Coles County, 1876-1976, was co-edited with Marta Ladd and the second, The Pictorial Landscape History of Charleston, Illinois, was co-authored and edited with Douglas K. Meyer.

Note: 'By the Bird's Song', 'An Apple for Clara', 'Hide and Seek' and the 'Sparrow and the Hawk' are excerpts from a longer work in progress.

Colophon

The typeset and layout were created on a Macintosh IIci with Microsoft 4.0C and New Century Schoolbook font. The original manuscript was printed on Hammermill Laser Plus paper using an Apple LaserWriter II NT. Frank Scott's graphics were scanned with a Hewlett Packard ScanJet Plus using Desk Scan Software. The graphics were sized and prepared for printing with Adlus FreeHand.

The text was printed on 70# patina matte finish by Phillips Brothers in Springfield, Illinois. The cover was printed and film laminated on Kivar 9, 10pt stock. The book was smythe sewn and bound over .092 binder board by R & R Bindery in Virden, Illinois